002937

F
Are        Arensen, Shel
              The CarJackers

6.00p

| | | DATE DUE | |
|---|---|---|---|
| | | | |
| | | | |
| | | | |
| | | | |
| | | | |
| | | | |
| | | | |
| | | | |
| | | | |
| | | | |

**THE RUGENDO RHINOS SERIES**

# THE CARJACKERS

## SHEL ARENSEN

Kregel
Publications

*The Carjackers*

© 2003 by Shel Arensen

Published by Kregel Publications, a division of Kregel, Inc., P.O. Box 2607, Grand Rapids, MI 49501.

Cover illustration: David Du

ISBN 0-8254-2042-3

Printed in the United States of America

03  04  05  06  07 / 5  4  3  2  1

*To my son Blake who,*
*together with his brothers and Bryan Adkins,*
*decided to try bike diving into the Little Gilgil River*
*near our house at Naivasha.*

# CHAPTER ONE

# THE STOLEN TRUCK

"**W**hat a great air pistol, Matt!" I stroked the curved wooden handle.

Matt smiled as he showed his new weapon off to the rest of our Rugendo Rhinos club. "It shoots pips—metal pellets—just like our air rifles," he explained, "but I can pump it up to twenty times to get more power!" He grabbed the pistol from me and pumped furiously. He grunted as he reached fifteen pumps. "It's a bit hard to keep pumping it after fifteen," he said.

He settled for seventeen and leaned out the window of our tree house. Steadying his right elbow with his left hand, he aimed at one of the small fruits in the wild fig tree where we Rhinos had built the tree house. Gently he squeezed the trigger and plastered a fruit into bits. He grinned.

"Great shot, Matt," Jon exclaimed. "Can I have a try?"

"Maybe later," Matt answered. "I want to be the first to bag a pigeon with my new gun today. Now let's get this meeting over so we can go hunting."

"I'll take roll," I suggested.

"Dean, you're such a genius!" Matt said in a mocking tone. "I say we skip roll call. We're all here. Anyone can see that!"

Since there were only four of us in our Rugendo Rhinos club I had to agree with Matt, but as the secretary, it was my job to call roll. I'm Dean Sandler, and though I'm six inches taller than Matt, I'm only in fifth grade. My dad edits a Christian magazine, so I was elected club secretary to call roll and keep notes of our meetings. Dad even helps me to write up some of our adventures.

I could see from the way Matt's trigger finger kept twitching he was so eager to try out his new gun on a pigeon hunt that he wouldn't be bothered with things like club rules today. Matt Chadwick, messy blond hair falling onto his forehead and sometimes covering his ice-blue eyes, is in sixth grade, the oldest guy in our club. As our club captain, when he orders us around, we hop. Matt's dad teaches Kenyan pastors in the Bible school at the Rugendo mission station high up in the forested highlands of central Kenya.

"Why have club rules if we never follow them?" asked Dave Krenden, his black-rimmed glasses tilted askew on his nose. As club treasurer Dave keeps track of our club dues. He's careful and cautious about everything. His dad is the building supervisor at the Rugendo mission station, which is why we put Dave in charge of building our tree fort in the ravine. Dave is in fourth grade together with Jon Freedman.

"I'm with Matt," Jon put in. "The sooner we go hunting, the sooner Matt can pot a pigeon and I'll get a chance to try out the new pistol." Jon had fallen in love with Africa when his parents moved to Rugendo just a few months before. His dad is a doctor at the hospital.

Matt rubbed the barrel of his new pistol on his baggy khaki shorts. "I don't really think we have any club business today," he said, "but if rules are important, Dean, go ahead and count heads and let's go hunting." Jon hopped up and was already halfway down our rope ladder before I could even stand up.

Jon had a gift for tracking animals. He could slip through the forest like a ghost, eyes keen to any signs that an animal had passed by. We sometimes joked and told him he was really a Dorobo, a member of a tribe of hunters that live in small villages scattered throughout Kenya's forests. We met a real Dorobo hunter in an earlier adventure, and Jon learned a passel of new tricks as the Dorobo took us tracking a bushbuck through the woods.

Matt stuffed his pistol deep into his pocket, and taking the rope ladder in both hands, he leaped out the door. I looked at Dave. He shrugged, and we both laughed. Hunting in the forest was our favorite club activity, rivaled only by riding our bikes. Dave stopped at the bottom of the tree and hid our rope ladder in a crotch of the massive wild fig.

Jon let out a whoop. "Bushbuck tracks," he called from his position bent down on one knee, peering at the damp forest soil that smelled of rotting leaves.

Matt joined him. "You're good, you old Dorobo, but today it's pigeons I'm after. Let's go to the river above Stanley Falls."

"I learned the Maasai word for pigeon or dove," I said, catching up with Matt and Jon. Dad had taken a deep interest in the Dorobo hunters, and since many of them spoke Maasai, my dad devoted some of his spare time to learning the Maasai language. "The Dorobo call a dove *enturrukuluo*."

Matt looked at me strangely. "That's a weird word."

"My dad says it's onomatopoetic for the sound a dove makes," I explained.

"Onoma who?" Matt asked. "Where do you learn such big words?"

I bit my lip in embarrassment. I didn't want the others thinking I was a nerdy brainer. "Onomatopoeia," I explained. "It means any word that sounds like what it describes. To the Dorobo and Maasai a dove in the trees sounds like it's saying, '*Enturrukuluo, enturrukuluo, enturrukuluo.*'"

Jon perked up. "That's what a dove sounds like when it's cooing."

I nodded. "So the Maasai word for dove comes from the sound it makes. Kind of like the Kikuyu name for Thomson's Falls— *Nyahururu*. That's the sound the water makes when it falls over the cliff. And words like that are onomatopoetic."

"That really is interesting," Matt said. It seemed like he really meant it. "But it won't help me bag a pigeon, so let's go." I'd tried before to explain to Matt that the ring-necked doves we hunted were not really pigeons, but he always called them pigeons. I didn't want to be too much of a scholar today. Matt ran ahead, carrying his pistol in his right hand.

As we approached a large open area near the river, I could hear the call of a dove. Matt and Jon heard it too. Matt stopped and pulled a pip from under his tongue and stuffed it into his pistol. He started pumping power into the gun, but before he'd even done three pumps, the plump dove flew off in a wild flapping of wings.

"I guess I'd better not wait until I see a pigeon before I pump my pistol," Matt said, a bit embarrassed at having scared off the bird so quickly. He pumped again. Jon reported the dove had settled in the branches of a pencil-cedar tree.

Jon and Matt crawled toward it. Dave and I stayed back to watch.

As Matt reached a man-sized bush, he hid behind it. He carefully aimed his pistol, using one of the branches to steady his barrel. We heard the shot, and the dove tumbled out of the tree. "I got him!" Matt shouted.

Jon ran ahead and grabbed the dove as it scrabbled around in the dirt. Taking the bird's body firmly in his right hand, Jon gave it a sharp whipping motion like when my mom shook down the mercury in the thermometer before taking my temperature. The dove's head separated from its body and flew into the bushes.

"That was a great shot," I congratulated Matt.

"I knew this pistol would be great!" Matt beamed. He hunkered down to help Jon who had already started plucking the soft gray feathers from the dove's plump breast. Dave collected some twigs to start a fire. I helped him and soon we had a nice pile. Dave pulled out a box of Zebra matches from his pocket. He bent down and lit some of the tinder and blew on it steadily until he had a good fire going.

Jon finished plucking and gutting the dove while Matt sent Dave and me to cut some green sticks for roasting the meat. We carefully chose a sturdy *leleshwa* bush with silvery-gray bark. The Maasai use *leleshwa* bushes for many things. They use the leaves for carrying fresh meat, the sticks for roasting, and make long-lasting campfires from gnarled *leleshwa* roots.

We skewered pigeon parts on our peeled sticks. As the smell of roasting bird filled my nostrils, I felt thirsty. "I need a drink," I said. "I'm going to the river." Dave joined me.

"Don't take too long," Matt teased. "There may not be any pigeon meat left by the time you come back."

We hurried to the river that started in a clear spring from the rocks in the steep mountainside behind us. The river dropped as waterfalls over a series of cliffs on its descent to the parched valley below. I could see the jagged rim of a volcanic crater that capped a rugged mountain rising from the valley floor. As I knelt down to scoop up some of the cold water, I noticed a gleam of white behind some bushes on the other side of the river. I drank and stood up. "What's that over there?" I asked Dave.

Dave wiped water off his chin and peered into the bushes. "I don't know. Maybe a piece of paper."

"I don't think so," I said, balancing on some rocks to cross the river for a closer look.

"I don't want to miss the meat," Dave said. "Come on, let's go."

"Just let me check it out," I said. I pushed my way through the bushes. I couldn't believe what I saw!

"Dave," I called, "it's a truck!"

"Give me a break," Dave shouted back. "What would a truck be doing here?"

"I don't know, but that's what it is," I said. I came back across the rocks. "Let's go get the others." We ran back to the fire and found Matt and Jon already chewing on the roast meat.

"You're almost too late," Matt said. He handed over a few juicy pieces.

"I saw a truck on the other side of the river," I told him as I took my chunk of the dove.

Matt gulped down his share. "What do you mean, a truck?"

"It's a white Isuzu lorry, the type that comes around and carries potatoes to the market in Nairobi," I said.

"Why would anyone dump an old truck down here?" Matt asked. "Are you sure you really saw a truck, Dean?"

"I'm sure, and it wasn't an old truck. The license plate started with KAH so that means it was licensed recently."

"Well, let's go see this truck of yours." Matt licked his fingers. Jon crunched on dove bones. He believed in eating every part of the doves we shot.

We pushed through the bushes to where I'd seen the truck. "You're right, Dean, this is a truck," said Matt.

"Maybe we could drive it home," I suggested.

Dave walked to the front. "No chance," he announced. "This truck has been stripped." He opened the hood. "See, they've taken the engine and every part that could be taken apart quickly. There aren't even any tires on it. It looks like someone stole the truck and took as many spares as possible to sell later. My dad says there's a big market for spare parts, and this way the thieves can't be traced."

"I guess we won't drive it home," Matt said sadly, "but we'd better tell our dads so they can report it to the police." He looked at me. "You did a good job, Dean. You discovered a stolen truck."

I returned the compliment. "And you shot a pigeon with your new pistol."

"Hey, I never got a chance to shoot your pistol," Jon complained. "Can I give it a try on our way home?"

"We better hurry," Dave said, pointing at dark clouds on the mountain above Rugendo. "It's going to rain soon."

"Later," Matt promised, and we rushed for home. We went to Dave's house first and told his dad about the truck. He agreed to report it to the police.

"That worries me if car thieves are operating so close to Rugendo," he said, getting into his Land Rover. Just then the first fat drops of rain started to fall. Within minutes the rain poured down like a waterfall, and we all dove into Dave's house for cover. His mom put on a video.

After about half an hour the rain started to let up. Dave looked out the window. "Hey, look at that!" he shouted.

# CHAPTER TWO

# THE CHURCH HARAMBEE

We all ran to the rain-beaded window to see what Dave was yelling about. "Flying ants!" Matt shouted. He flung open the door. "Let's catch some!" We followed him. Dave came last, carrying an empty Blue Band margarine tub to collect the ants.

Jon went frantic, batting the ants out of the air and pouncing on them before dropping them into the tub. The flying ants are large termites that come out of holes in the ground after big rains when the water floods out their underground homes. They use their four two-inch-long, see-through wings to fly around for an hour or two. They have fat, pale-tan bodies about the size of a jelly bean. They would soon lose their wings and scurry back to their underground city—except for those we Rhinos caught and ate.

Matt didn't put many into the container. He was too busy eating them raw. Pinching off the four wings, he'd pop the wriggling flying ant in his mouth and crunch it between his teeth before swallowing. I wasn't quite so brave, but I really liked them fried. They tasted slightly like peanuts, mostly like a glob of salty butter. That might have been because my recipe for cooking flying ants involved frying them in lots of butter and salt. As Matt got full of raw flying ants he started putting ants in our container.

Soon the container, big enough to hold two pounds of margarine, was full of writhing ants, and we headed back to Dave's kitchen. His mom handed us an old camping skillet. "Use this one," she said. "And try not to burn the bottom of the pan this time."

As Dave melted the butter, we stripped off wings and started dropping the flying ants into the frying pan. "Look, more are coming for the feast," I said. Flying ants, attracted to the lights in the house, bumped into the window and crawled under the door. I gathered the termites off the floor to fill our frying pan.

Soon the feast was ready. We sat down in front of the fireplace and scooped up fried flying ants by the spoonful. Some of the ants had fried longer on the bottom of the pan and had turned a crunchy brown. Those were my favorite. We quickly polished them off. "That was good stuff," Matt said, a trace of shiny butter on his chin.

"Well, I'd better get home," I said. Jon and Matt agreed, so we said good-bye to Dave and thanked his mom for letting us cook our flying ant feast in her kitchen.

"You're welcome, boys," she said. "We'll see you tomorrow at church. Remember they're having a *harambee* after the service."

At home I told my parents about finding the stolen truck. Mom was too busy fixing Swedish pancakes to pay much attention to my story, but my dad listened. "Car theft is becoming more and more common in this country," he said. "Here, help me set the table."

At supper I felt full after eating six Swedish pancakes, thin plate-sized pancakes that I smeared with butter and sprinkled with sugar.

"Are you all right?" my mom asked. "I've never known you to eat less than twelve!"

"More for me," my little brother, Craig, said around a big bite of pancake. He smiled.

"I'm not sick," I said. "Just full. It must have been all those flying ants we ate at Dave's house."

"Flying ants!" my mom said. "No wonder you're not hungry. You're probably feeling sick from eating those disgusting bugs." Her head gave a sideways shudder, and she closed her eyes.

"I'm not sick from the flying ants," I said. "They were good. I just ate too many, but your pancakes are extra good tonight, so I'll have another." That satisfied my mom so she wouldn't take my temperature and all that stuff.

At devotions Dad read the story of Ruth and how she'd left her family and country to follow her mother-in-law. When it was time to pray, he asked me to remember the church *harambee*. "What's the *harambee* for?" I asked.

"It's to raise money for the roof of a new church about five miles from here at a place called Mugwanja," Dad said. "Some of the church elders from here at Rugendo have been going out to this place doing house-to-house evangelism. As people accepted Christ, they started meeting under a tree. The new believers decided to build a wooden church, and the Rugendo church wants to help buy the iron roofing sheets."

We prayed for the *harambee,* and after taking a bath I went to bed to read.

The next day after breakfast Brad, a short-term missionary who worked at Dad's magazine as a graphic designer, came over. "What's this *harambee* thing, anyway?" Brad asked.

"*Harambee* is a Swahili word that was used to encourage people to pull together," Dad said. "It used to be if a car got stuck in the mud, you'd call some people. They'd get a rope and, in order to get everyone to pull at the same moment to maximize the power, they would shout, '*HaramBEE*,' with an emphasis on the last syllable. As they shouted out the last syllable, which is pronounced 'bay,' they would all heave on the rope and pull the car out of the mud."

"But there won't be any cars stuck in the mud at church, Dad," I joked.

He laughed. "No, you're right. The first president of Kenya, Mzee Jomo Kenyatta, used the word to encourage everyone to pull together in nation building. And whenever there was a community fund-raiser they would call it a *harambee* where everyone was expected to join in and give to help out. Now any fund-raiser is called a *harambee*."

"Sounds interesting," Brad said. "At first I thought it was just a way to force the missionaries to give more."

Dad smiled. "Not all missionaries like *harambees*. Often there is a lot of showy giving and applause for the big givers, which kind of goes against Jesus' teaching where he said we shouldn't announce our giving with trumpets so other people would praise us. I look on it as an African celebration of giving. The money is going to the Lord's work."

"I like *harambees*," I cut in, "because Dad gives me lots of coins to spend on buying fruit and other things."

Dad nodded and went on. "The *harambee* becomes a fun event for giving. Here's some advice I received from an old Kenyan pastor. Decide what you want to give in total, but don't give it all at once. Bring your money in lots of small shilling notes and coins."

"That reminds me, Dad," I cut in. "I need money to buy some loquats at the *harambee*." I loved the tart yellow fruit.

Dad handed me five ten-shilling coins. "If you bring loose cash, you can take part in the auctions and other giving events without feeling you're forced to give more than you planned. You'll give the amount you planned to give, which is biblical. Paul said each man should give what he has decided in his heart. Have fun! This is Kenya and a *harambee* is Kenyan-style giving."

The church service lasted the usual two hours with lots of testimonies and songs. The only thing different was that the front of the church looked like a market. There was a stalk of green bananas, chickens with their feet tied, baskets covered with intricately crocheted doilies, a cake, a banana tree, green pumpkins, sugarcane stalks, and much more. I spied several bags of yellow loquats.

When the service finally ended, the pastor asked us to stay for the *harambee* to raise money for the roof at the new Mugwanja church. "After the *harambee* there will be lunch served of *mugimo* and stew."

I loved *mugimo,* a mash of potatoes and beans and hard corn kernels. It usually included pumpkin leaves as well, which turned the mash bright green. My stomach rumbled as I thought of grabbing a handful of *mugimo* and dipping it in the savory meat and cabbage stew, but for now I had to wait and watch the *harambee.*

I went and sat next to my friend, Kamau, near the front. I shook his hand and asked, "What are you going to buy in the auction? I want at least one of those bags of loquats."

Kamau jingled some coins in his hand. "I haven't decided what to bid on."

Kamau's father, called Baba Kamau, was one of the church elders, and he served as the master of ceremonies for the *harambee*. First he welcomed all of us. "Everybody must greet me in the air," he said, wanting us to wave our hands at him in greeting. We all did.

"All right," Baba Kamau said, "all those who greeted me need to greet me again with five shillings." All the Kenyans were delighted at the way Kamau's father had gotten everyone involved so quickly, and they streamed to the front and shook his hand and dropped five-shilling coins in the woven *kiondo* basket.

My dad passed by and shoved a five-shilling piece into my hand. I followed him to the front and shook Baba Kamau's hand and dropped my five shillings into the colorful woven basket. As I turned, I bumped into a girl from my class at school. I blushed. Jill was really pretty—for a girl. Her friends Rachel and Rebekah stood behind her. They lived in the dorm at school because their parents worked as missionaries translating the Bible in Zaire.

A crowd of people squeezed the girls up the aisle as I pushed my way back to my seat. I only had time to nod a greeting, but my stomach churned when Jill smiled at me.

"I told you Dean liked Jill," Rachel whispered to Rebekah as we passed. I hurried to my pew.

Next, Baba Kamau asked who wanted old Mr. Bailey, the oldest missionary at Rugendo, to sing a song. It was a well-known fact the Mr. Bailey had a terrible froglike voice, but he loved to sing loudly. He beamed as many people put up their hands. Baba Kamau went on, "All those who want Mr. Bailey to sing should put five shillings in the basket." Over twenty people went up and put their money in the basket. Baba Kamau counted the money.

"We have 140 shillings for Mr. Bailey to sing us a song." Mr. Bailey stood up. Baba Kamau said, "If anyone doesn't want Mr. Bailey to sing right now, they have to put in more than 140 shillings."

My mom stood up and waved a 200 shilling note. "Two hundred shillings for Mr. Bailey not to sing," she said. Everyone laughed. Mr. Bailey pretended to be disappointed and started to sit down.

Baba Kamau reached into his pocket and put down 100 shillings. "I want to hear Mr. Bailey sing," he said. "Can anyone help me with more money to top Mama Dean's bid of 200 shillings to stop the singing?" People popped up and soon 210 shillings had been donated. This went back and forth until almost 1,000 shillings had been raised when, finally, Mr. Bailey stood up and croaked out the first line of "Amazing Grace" in Kikuyu.

This was followed by donations from various groups that had been invited to the *harambee*. It seemed that every church in the district had sent a delegation. Finally, all the market items were auctioned off. I bought two bags of loquats for my fifty shillings and gave one bag to Kamau. Mr. Njogu, the editor at the magazine, bought a chicken for 300 shillings and gave it to my dad. He gave it back to be auctioned again after my mom punched him in the ribs.

"Doesn't your mother want the chicken?" whispered Kamau.

"She doesn't like plucking a chicken," I answered. "She prefers to buy them already butchered at the shop."

"You Americans are strange," Kamau commented. His father auctioned a stalk of sugarcane and Kamau bought it.

When the *harambee* ended, Baba Kamau announced that we had raised 30,000 shillings (about $400), more than enough to buy the iron sheets for the Mugwanja church. He asked Mama Paul to give an announcement about how the food would be served, and she prayed for the meal.

Kamau and I found the other Rhinos, and we sat on a bench to eat our *mugimo* and stew together. We didn't talk much, as we were too busy stuffing our faces.

"I have a riddle," I heard a voice say. I turned to see Jill, Rachel, and Rebekah sitting behind us. Rachel smirked. "Why do Rhinos eat like pigs?"

Matt glared at the girls. "I think I know the answer," Rebekah said. "Because they are pigs?"

Matt put a wad of *mugimo* in his spoon and pulled it back as if he would flick it at the girls. "Not here in the church hall, Matt," Dave protested. "Just ignore them."

Brad sat down next to us and said to my dad who stood nearby, "You were right. That really was a cultural way of giving. Thanks for your advice. I had lots of small shilling notes and a good time giving. I even bought a banana tree to plant at my house!"

After our meal, Kamau borrowed a knife from the church kitchen and whacked off six-inch lengths of sugarcane joints and gave them to each of us Rhinos. He thanked me for the loquats, and followed his dad toward their home. We Rhinos chewed off chunks of sugarcane, sucked out the juice, and spit out the straw-like remains by the roadside as we walked home. I shared my bag of loquats. Matt devoured the fruit and pulled out the shiny brown pits that were the size of marbles. Pinching a seed, he squeezed it out of his fingers. It flew into Dave's ear.

"Ow! That hurt!" Dave howled. He bit into a loquat and pulled out the pit. He hurled it at Matt, who ducked. The pit hit an old

Kenyan man passing by on the road. He frowned at us. "I'm sorry," Dave apologized to the old man.

I munched a shallow bite into the yellow flesh of a loquat, revealing the glistening seeds. There were three. I pulled them out with my tongue and spit them into my hand. "Let's have a contest to see who can find the most seeds in one loquat," I suggested. Dave won the contest with a massive five-pit loquat.

The next morning before school I heard a knock on the door. I opened it to find Kamau. "Where's your father?" Kamau asked, pushing his way into the house.

My dad came out of his room. "What's the matter?" he asked.

"The money from the *harambee* was stolen last night." Kamau was on the verge of tears. "And they're saying my father is the one who took it!"

# CHAPTER THREE

# THE CARJACKERS STRIKE!

**M**y dad promised Kamau he would go down to the police post where Baba Kamau had been taken for questioning. Just then Brad walked into the house. "Did I leave my bug here last night?" he asked.

"What bug?" Dad asked, his face wrinkled into a puzzled frown.

"My car," Brad explained. "My Volkswagen bug. I thought I'd parked it outside my house, but it wasn't there this morning. Maybe I drove it over here last night when I had that question about the new logo for the Problem Post column in the magazine."

"It's not here, Brad," I said. "Are you sure it didn't roll down your driveway and into someone's garden?" Brad's old VW bug was a joke around Rugendo. Only one headlight worked and the emergency brake never held. The battery usually didn't hold a charge, so Brad often left it on hills so he could roll-start the car. Even though Dad said Brad was a very talented graphic designer, he was terribly messy and always forgot where he put things.

"I'm sure your VW bug will show up, Brad," Dad said. "It's so battered I doubt anyone would steal it. Anyway, I'll be late at the office. I'm going down to the police post to check on a report that yesterday's *harambee* money was stolen and Baba Kamau has been taken in for questioning."

I looked at the clock and grabbed my books and ran. School started in ten minutes, and I had a long way to go—all uphill!

At recess I found the other Rhinos. "Did you hear about the *harambee* money being stolen?" I asked. "And Brad can't find his car!"

Matt laughed. "That guy would lose his eyeballs if God hadn't fastened them into his head."

At chapel one of the teachers reminded us about the hobby show the next Friday. I had signed up to show my shell collection. Dave had been working hard on some model airplanes. Even Jon had a new hobby. His dad had taken him fishing, so Jon decided to show off fishing as his hobby.

"I have a special surprise as part of my speech," Jon whispered to me from the row in front. His teacher gave him a hard glare for whispering during the principal's announcement. Jon turned around quickly.

That night Dad was late for supper. When he came in, his face looked like a sad old wildebeest. "What's wrong, honey?" my mom asked. He sat down heavily on the couch.

"Is Baba Kamau in big trouble?" I wanted to know.

He waved off my question. "No. In a case like this the police usually blame the person who had the money rather than looking for the real thieves, but they let Baba Kamau go for lack of any proof." He sighed. "I just got back from the big police post near Kiambu. I had to go get Dr. Freedman."

"Doesn't he have a new Land Rover?" my mom asked. "Why couldn't he drive himself?"

"Because his Land Rover was stolen this afternoon at gunpoint," Dad said grimly.

"What happened?" I asked. I sat down next to him, a chill of fear tickling the back of my neck.

"He was driving up the hill above Rugendo to check on one of the small clinics. He had to slow down at that hairpin bend just above the spot where the Rugendo River forms that pretty waterfall."

I nodded. We often went on hikes to the waterfall. "As he slowed down two men stepped out of the forest carrying pistols. They wrenched open his door, pointed the gun at his head, and forced him to drive away. They directed him to an isolated road that goes through the Gatamayu forest. Once there they took him out, tied him to a tree, and drove off with the Land Rover." He stopped and shook his head. "This country is getting dangerous," he said. "Those robbers carjacked Dr. Freedman in broad daylight!"

"How did Dr. Freedman get to the police?" I asked.

"He'd held his wrists slightly apart when they tied him up," Dad explained. "Once the robbers left, he managed to wriggle his hands free and untied himself from the tree. He walked to the road and flagged down a passing car." Dad rubbed his temples. "We're having a security meeting at Dr. Freedman's in half an hour. We're going to thank God for protecting him and decide what we can do about the problem."

Mom warmed up a plate of spaghetti for Dad. He left with a worried look on his face. My mother gave me a hug. I squeezed extra hard, not wanting to let go of her. Robbers with guns had stolen a Land Rover right here at Rugendo! My world didn't seem safe as I went to bed.

The next day when I got to school a knot of kids surrounded

Jon. I stood on the outside of the crowd and looked over their heads as he told how his dad had been held up at gunpoint. "My dad held his wrists in a locked-out position so he could escape easily," Jon boasted.

The first bell for school rang, and the kids headed off for class. We Rhinos moved up close to Jon. "Sorry about your dad losing the Land Rover," Matt said. "It was a cool car." He punched Jon gently on the shoulder.

Jon just smiled. "Yeah, I'll miss that car." He stopped and looked serious. "I'm just really glad my dad wasn't hurt. Those guys had guns."

We hurried to class. At recess Dave and I agreed that after school we'd meet at his house, and I'd work on mounting some of my seashells on a board while he painted some of his model airplanes.

"I'm going home to practice for my speech about fishing," Jon said. He had a mysterious smile on his face, and I wondered what he meant. I just couldn't imagine Jon spending a lot of time memorizing.

Matt looked disgusted. "Well, I guess I'll have the afternoon to myself. I don't have any hobbies. Too boring."

At Dave's house I took a piece of hardboard, which I'd painted light blue, and began arranging my cowries—shiny, wildly patterned shells I'd collected on Kenya's coastal reefs in the Indian Ocean. I put the larger shells, like the tortoise cowrie, the tiger cowrie, and the map cowrie, on the bottom. The medium-sized cowries, like the lynx cowrie, went in the middle of the board. I put the tiny cowries, like the kitten cowrie and dawn cowrie, at the top. I glued the shells on with a kind of glue that could easily be peeled off later. My mom had given me some labels, and I wrote the names of each shell carefully and glued them underneath the different species of cowries. As I worked, Dave patiently painted camouflage paint on his now-completed model of a British mosquito bomber from World War 2.

Suddenly Matt and Jon burst in. "Guess what!" Matt said. Before either of us could guess, Matt told us that the men on the mission station had decided everyone should have security alarms put on their cars. "There's a guy from Nairobi right now attaching one to Mr. Rayford's car," he went on. Mr. Rayford was the principal of our missionary kids' school.

"Let's go watch them put it on," Dave said. He almost knocked over his model airplane in his hurry. We ran out the door and soon stood outside Mr. Rayford's house watching the mechanic. He had the hood of the Peugeot 504 up and was running wires in and out. He opened the front door and crawled underneath the steering wheel. Finally he grunted and said, "It's all set. Now let's test it." He locked the door of the car and jerked on the handle. Immediately the car alarm began to emit metallic-sounding whistles and piercing sirens. We all covered out ears and turned away. Mr. Rayford smiled. "If anyone tries to steal my car at night, I'll know about it," he said.

"Actually," the mechanic said, "this alarm will wake you up, but it will do nothing to stop a thief from starting your car and driving away. I would suggest you also put on an immobilizer, which cuts off the electrical supply, making it impossible to start the car. Or perhaps you could put a crook-lock on the gearshift."

Mr. Rayford looked annoyed. "I'm sure you just want more of my business. I've paid you quite enough, and I don't think those extra gimmicks are really needed."

The mechanic shrugged and packed his tools. We wandered off leaving Mr. Rayford rubbing his hands and looking lovingly at his Peugeot.

Just then Brad walked up the road. "You guys haven't seen my bug anywhere?" he asked. "I'm sure I parked it outside my house. But you never know. I could have parked it at the top of a hill for an easy start in the morning, and it might have rolled away." He looked at me. "Like you said this morning." We walked around with him checking all the possible places his Volkswagen could have rolled into.

"Maybe it started itself and drove away like Herbie, the Love Bug," Matt suggested. We all laughed, even Brad.

Brad shook his head. "This is crazy. The car isn't anywhere. I'm sure it must have been stolen."

Jon said, "Maybe, but I think the thieves are usually after nicer cars, like my dad's new Land Rover."

"Or that truck we found on Saturday over by the river," I put in.

"You found a truck by the river?" Brad asked.

Matt explained about the truck we'd seen that had obviously been stolen and stripped of all usable parts for sale on the used parts market.

"I think that's what happened to my car!" Brad exclaimed. "It may not have been worth much as a car, but I'll bet someone stole it to sell the parts."

"I'm not so sure, Brad," Dave said with a frown. "I don't think your car had many good parts left in it."

Brad ignored Dave's comment and asked, "Can you show me where you found that truck? Maybe it's the place where they hide all the stolen cars and take them apart. Maybe we'll even find Dr. Freedman's Land Rover there."

"It's getting dark now," said Matt, "but we can show you the place tomorrow after school."

We said good-bye to Brad, and Matt challenged us to a race to his house. We sprinted down the road in a bunch. As we passed by Mr. Rayford's house, Matt darted across the lawn heading for a shortcut he knew. His turn surprised the rest of us, and Matt had a good lead by the time we also shifted direction and cut through Mr. Rayford's yard. Matt looked back to see if we were catching up with him and bumped into Mr. Rayford's Peugeot. The car alarm burst into action with its wailing siren and hiccuping hoots of the horn.

"Let's get out of here," Matt said as we sprinted out of the yard.

# CHAPTER FOUR

# THE HOBBY SHOW

**W**ith Mr. Rayford's car alarm blaring in our ears, we Rhinos scattered, each of us sprinting for his own house. I arrived home breathless, threw open the door, and slammed it behind me. "Are you all right, Dean?" my mom asked with a puzzled look on her face.

I nodded and ran upstairs to my room. The telephone rang. Some years before, a town in America had purchased a new telephone exchange. No one knew what to do with the old telephones. Someone suggested maybe the old telephone exchange and the dial phones could be helpful to some mission station. The exchange was shipped out to Rugendo and some technicians wired it up so everyone on the station could call each other. Dad picked up the phone. I heard him say, "Why, hello, Mr. Rayford. What can I do for you?" He paused and said in an agitated voice, "What? I'll be right over!" He put the phone down. "I might be late for supper again," he called to my mom. "It seems some thieves tried to get Mr. Rayford's car, but the alarm went off and scared them away." The door opened and shut with a bang.

I sat down on my bed with a sinking feeling in my stomach,

kind of like when the elevator stopped on the fourth floor at Mansion House in Nairobi before my dental appointment. I knew I should tell my dad we had set off the alarm, but I didn't want to get Matt in trouble.

"Craig and Dean," Mom called, "it's time for supper." I slowly walked to the dining room. "Dad will be a bit late," my mom informed us. "Some car thieves tried to get Mr. Rayford's car just now."

I sat down. I fumbled with my carved wooden rhino napkin ring and knocked it on the floor.

"Are you sure you're all right, Dean?" my mom asked as she set down a plate of steaming rice and stir-fried vegetables.

"Uh, yeah, of course," I answered. "Why do you keep asking?"

"I know you, son," she said, "and I know something funny is going on. First you come running into the house and into your room without even asking what's for supper. Now you're shaking and you dropped your napkin ring. And your face tells me you're hiding something. So out with it. Are you in trouble at school?"

"Oh, no," I said. "Honest, Mom, everything's fine."

Mom stared hard at me, and I knew she didn't believe me. However, she dropped the subject, and after a short prayer we started to eat.

"What did you find out, dear?" Mom asked, when Dad walked in.

"Not much," he replied. "There didn't seem to be any type of attempted break-in on the car. The alarm is set to go off at the slightest touch. Anyway, Dr. Freedman and Mr. Rayford are going down to the police post to report the situation and ask the police to be alert."

I looked at my food and found I wasn't hungry at all. Dad noticed at once that I wasn't eating. "Are you sick, Dean?" he asked. "Why aren't you eating?"

I knew I'd have to tell. "There's really no need for them to go to the police, Dad," I said.

"Why not?" he demanded with a stern frown.

"Because Matt . . . or I should say . . . uh, we set off the alarm on Mr. Rayford's car." I explained how Matt had bumped into the car. "The siren from the car alarm scared us so much that we all ran away."

Dad put his big hand on my shoulder and squeezed. "Come with me," he said. He marched me out of the house and up the path to Mr. Rayford's yard. Mr. Rayford and Dr. Freedman were just getting into the Peugeot to go to the police post. As Mr. Rayford put the key in the door and turned it, the siren shrieked again. "Oh dear! Oh dear!" Mr. Rayford fumbled with his jumble of keys to find the new button to turn off the alarm. Drops of sweat had already formed on his forehead by the time he switched off the hideous noise.

"I'm glad we caught you," Dad said. "Dean has something to tell you."

Mr. Rayford looked down at me. "Yes?" he questioned.

"Uh, did you see how easily you set off your alarm just now?" I began.

"Yes. What's the point, Dean?" he asked, his eyebrows puckering.

"Well, we Rhinos, that is . . . Matt, Dave, Jon, and me . . ."

"I," corrected Mr. Rayford.

"Right, well, anyway, we were running along through your yard, and Matt bumped the front fender of your car and the alarm went off. The noise really startled us—kind of like it did you just now—

and we ran off. We should have come right to you. I'm sorry for running away and letting you think thieves were trying to steal your car."

"Well," Mr. Rayford said kindly, "at least I won't have to spend my evening at the police post writing out a statement. You boys should be more careful in the future."

"Yes, Mr. Rayford," I answered.

"I'll have a word with Jon when I get home," Dr. Freedman said. "And I'll talk to Matt's and Dave's parents as well. With all the worry over carjackers, you boys really need to watch your step."

I walked home with my dad, his arm on my shoulder. "Do you feel better now?" he asked.

"Yeah," I answered. "And now I'm hungry!"

The next day after school we Rhinos gathered at Matt's house. "Did you get in trouble?" I asked Dave.

"Just a lecture," Dave answered.

"Me, too," said Matt. Jon nodded.

Matt went on. "Let's go get Brad and look for his Volkswagen at the river."

After a quick hike through the bush we reached the river and showed Brad the stripped-down Isuzu truck.

"I'm sure my car's around here somewhere," Brad said as we began searching the area in ever-widening circles. We found nothing. Not even Jon could find any signs of tire tracks.

Suddenly Brad squatted down and hissed, "I hear something." We all dropped and stared at the bushes where Brad pointed. At first all was silent, then a few branches moved and we all saw it.

"It's just a bushbuck," Jon declared. On hearing his voice, the secretive antelope darted away toward the river.

"I think we'd better head home," Matt said. "I'm sorry, Brad, but if your bug was stolen it wasn't hidden here."

"You're right," Brad said. "I'll have to report it stolen to the police and see if they ever find it."

The next day at school was the hobby show. We all set up our displays on tables in the school auditorium at lunchtime. After lunch everyone wandered up and down the aisles, checking out the displays. I walked around with the Rhinos. Dave had his model airplanes hanging from strings so they appeared to be in flight. As we admired Dave's planes, Jill, Rachel, and Rebekah sidled over.

"Where's your display, Matt?" Jill said. "I thought your hobby was solving mysteries."

Matt looked chuffed. "I'm glad you girls admit that my Rhino club is good at solving mysteries . . . ," Matt began.

"I guess there's nothing to display at the moment," Rachel put in. "Especially since the Rhinos haven't even been able to find out who stole Jon's Land Rover."

"That's not fair," Matt answered. "We're . . ."

The girls didn't stay to listen.

"Forget them, Matt," Jon advised. "Come see my display."

"This is cool," Matt said. He touched a brown fishing lure that looked like a crayfish. A fishing pole, a net, and a stuffed four-pound bass sat on a board with a map of Lake Naivasha painted on it. Jon had marked some Xs in front of Hippo Point and Crescent Island with dates and weights of fish he had caught at those places.

We wandered on. "Look," I pointed. "Jill's hobby is cooking." She had a lemon meringue pie and a plate of chocolate chip cookies made with large chunks of Cadbury dark chocolate bars. They smelled tempting, and I almost reached for one before I saw the sign that read, "Tasting for judges only."

Some kids had stamp collections, others had postcard collections, others had bottle tops, butterflies, gum wrappers, and baseball cards. Some kids said reading was their hobby and listed books they had read in the past year. The greatest collection belonged to a third grader who had built a city out of cardboard tubes from the inside of toilet paper rolls. He had a sign saying: "I collect cardboard toilet paper rolls because they are fun to build with." He had built a crazy-looking tube city with roads made from tubes he'd cut in half lengthwise. He'd placed matchbox cars as if they were driving along the roads. Another sign announced, "Toilet paper tube city. Population 48,000."

After the viewing, one of the teachers called everyone to sit down so we could hear the speeches. Each student with a hobby had to stand up and tell about his or her hobby. My stomach churned as I waited for my turn.

Jill's friend Rachel was first. "My hobby is stamp collecting, and I like my hobby because I learn about different countries of the world. My favorite stamps are these diamond-shaped stamps with beautiful flowers on them. They come from my home country, Zaire." She flashed the page of stamps at the audience and hurried off the stage.

Jon went next. He tramped up to the podium carrying his fishing pole.

"My hobby is fishing," Jon announced. "And this is how I cast." Pushing the thumb switch on his reel, he swung the pole back before whipping it forward. In his nervousness, Jon released the thumb catch too late, and instead of a straight cast down the aisle of the auditorium, Jon's line snaked out sideways, and the hookless lure on the end of his line thumped one of the judges on the shoulder. The judge jerked backwards in surprise. Jon's eyes widened. "Sorry," Jon apologized as he hastily reeled in his line. He waited for a reaction from the judge. "What would happen on the lake if you missed a cast like that?" the judge asked.

"When I make a bad cast, my dad helps me unhook my lure from a wad of papyrus," Jon answered warily.

The judge smiled. "Don't worry. Sometimes I cast into the papyrus as well," he said.

When it was my turn to give my speech, my stomach surged with a fluttering, nervous feeling, but once I'd said my first line, "I am a conchologist," I calmed down and explained that a conchologist was a shell collector. I showed off a large humpbacked cowrie and explained how I'd collected it from the cliffs at Ras Ngomeni on the Kenyan coast. I held up a tiny small-toothed cowrie, smaller than the fingernail on my pinkie. "I found this rare treasure underneath a slimy piece of rubble near the Likoni ferry," I said.

"The shells of Kenya's coast are disappearing because of over-collecting. I've learned the importance of putting back any shells that I already have in my collection. When I turn a rock over, I put it back carefully to protect the many sea creatures that use that rock as a home. And whenever I find a shell sitting on eggs, I leave it alone so the eggs can grow and become shells for others to see and enjoy."

After the speeches one of the teachers said, "There will now be a fifteen-minute break while the judges make their choices for the winners and runners-up. You are free to view the displays again while you wait.

Mr. Rayford, the principal, walked quickly to the platform and said, "After the winners are announced there will be a brief special meeting for kids whose parents work in Zaire." He rumpled a piece of paper in his hands as he talked and his face looked grim. I glanced nervously at Rachel and Rebekah who stood whispering to Jill.

# CHAPTER FIVE

# DANGER IN ZAIRE

One of the judges stood up and walked to the podium. She said the usual stuff about how everyone had worked so hard and all the hobbies were so good—she actually used the word *admirable*—that it was very hard for the judges to decide. The frilly-fluffy white ruffles in the center of the blouse under her navy blue coat quivered as she took a deep breath. "But we had to make some choices," she went on and announced that Ben, in first grade, had been the runner-up for his collection of Matchbox cars. Jill's little sister, Beth, won first prize for the first grade with her hobby of painting watercolors.

Thunderous clapping surrounded the two embarrassed first graders who leaned against each other for support as they walked forward to receive their ribbons—blue for first place, red for the runner-up.

The prize giving went on. In fourth grade Dave and Jon tied as the two best runners-up. Matt and I stood up as we cheered and clapped. Rachel had her arm around Rebekah. They didn't look very happy. I wondered what the meeting for Zaire kids was about.

"Now for the fifth grade," the judge's voice blared through the microphone. I forgot about Rachel and Rebekah for the moment. I knew my shell collection had a good chance for winning in the fifth grade, but my mouth went dry as the judge announced the runner-up. It wasn't me. I held my breath. "The winner for the fifth grade . . ." The judge paused. ". . . is Dean Sandler for his fascinating collection of seashells."

My head spun. I stood up and walked forward, my face turning red. I smiled a silly grin and waved my blue ribbon as I stepped off the stage.

When I sat down Matt pounded me on the back. "Good job, Dean! Maybe I should enter a hobby in the show sometime!" I didn't mention that since he was in sixth grade he'd just passed his last chance.

A hand tapped me on the shoulder. I looked back at Jill. "Good job," she whispered with a friendly smile.

"Sorry you didn't win a prize," I whispered back. "Your lemon meringue pie looked really juicy!" My words were lost in the clapping as the sixth grade winners were announced. Rachel Maxwell from Zaire won first prize with her stamp collection.

After the hobby show I saw Rachel and Rebekah and other kids whose parents worked in Zaire moving toward the front of the chapel where Mr. Rayford waited for them.

"Want some pie?" Jill asked as I picked up my board of shells.

I dug into the lemon meringue. The tart taste made my saliva glands curl, but I loved it. "This is really good!" I said. "You definitely should have won a prize." She smiled.

The Zaire students clustered around Mr. Rayford and I heard him begin, "I don't want to scare any of you, but the news from Zaire is not good. There's been a lot of rebel activity, and the government soldiers have fled. So most mission groups have decided to evacuate or move their missionaries out of Zaire."

My mom waited for me by the car. As I struggled to slide my shell board into the backseat, I asked her if she'd heard that missionaries were being evacuated from Zaire.

"Yes," she answered, opening the front door to help me pull the corner of the board over the rear seat cushion where it had caught.

Done, she stood up and said, "Your dad was called into Nairobi this morning for an emergency meeting of the mission leaders. We'll probably have to house a lot of the Zaire missionaries here at Rugendo."

I thought of Rachel and Rebekah. Their parents worked in Zaire. "Are the missionaries safe?" I asked.

Mom looked sad. "I don't know, Dean. They're in God's hands. I pray they'll all get out all right."

I didn't say anything as we drove home. It was hard to be excited about winning a blue ribbon when other kids' parents were in danger.

That evening my dad arrived home just before supper. The skin under his eyes sagged and looked ash gray, but he smiled when he saw me. "Hey, Dean, sorry I missed your hobby show. How'd you do?"

"I won first prize," I answered, pleased that he'd remembered the hobby show with all the Zaire stuff going on. "Are the Zaire missionaries going to be safe?" I asked.

"Yes," he assured me with a hand on my shoulder. He frowned. "Most of them, anyway."

"What do you mean?" I asked.

"I'll tell you later," he said as he walked in and saw the table set for supper. Mom came over quickly and gave Dad a hug. We sat down to eat.

"We're having an all-station prayer meeting at the school chapel starting at 7:30 this evening," Dad stated between mouthfuls. "We need to do some serious praying for Zaire. Not just for the missionaries, but for the church leaders who will be staying in the middle of the unrest."

He looked at me. "Mr. Rayford suggested the prayer meeting be at the school so all you kids could be involved in praying as well. I've been asked to bring an updated report."

After supper we drove up to the school chapel. "Save me a seat," Dad said. "I have to give Rachel and Rebekah some news before we announce it in the meeting for prayer." I saw my dad nod at Mr. Rayford, and the two took Rebekah and Rachel aside and talked in a whisper. I could tell by the way Rachel's shoulder sagged that it wasn't happy news. Students and staff filled every seat, but instead of the normal happy chatter, the room was as quiet as the missionary graveyard at the bottom of the hill where Matt's little sister had been buried after she died of malaria. Dad came back and sat next to me while Mr. Rayford walked to the pulpit and opened in prayer before asking my dad to fill everyone in on what had been happening in Zaire.

My dad cleared his throat and began, "Zaire's dictator has ruled that country quite harshly for the past thirty years or so. A group of rebel soldiers loyal to another leader has begun to sweep through eastern Zaire. The government soldiers have been so poorly paid in recent years that they had no reason to fight for the existing government, so they fled—often shooting and looting as they went.

"Yesterday when the rebels neared the area where many of our missionaries work, the mission leaders decided to move all the missionaries out of Zaire. Some missionaries who lived close to the border drove out through Uganda. Others were airlifted from strips near the mission stations."

I looked over to where Rachel and Rebekah Maxwell sat. They clung to each other and seemed to be crying.

"All missionaries but two have gotten out of Zaire safely," my dad went on. "The last two are Mr. Maxwell and a young single missionary, Jim Temple.

Rachel and Rebekah hugged each other tighter.

"Mr. Maxwell, as the team leader, refused to leave until he'd gotten all the others out safely. They were at the airstrip at one of our stations sending off the last group of missionaries. The plane was scheduled to land those missionaries across the border in Uganda yesterday afternoon and then return to pick up Mr. Maxwell and Jim Temple. But before the plane had gone very far, Mr. Maxwell called by radio to the pilot to say they could see soldiers arriving. He and Jim Temple planned to head for the Uganda border in a Land Cruiser." My dad paused. "We've heard nothing since."

Rachel sobbed, and Rebekah held her tight. Mr. Rayford and some others sat next to them to comfort them.

Dad went on, "I'm going to read some verses from the Psalms to encourage us that God will hear and answer our prayers."

He told us to open our Bibles to Psalm 40 verses one through three. He began to read, "'I waited patiently for the LORD; he turned to me and heard my cry. He lifted me out of the slimy pit, out of the mud and mire; he set my feet on a rock and gave me a firm place to stand. He put a new song in my mouth, a hymn of praise to our God. Many will see and fear and put their trust in the LORD.'"

Everyone broke up into small groups of five or six and began praying. Matt's dad led our group. "Let's pray first for God to protect Mr. Temple and Mr. Maxwell," he instructed.

"Lord, keep them safe," Matt prayed. Others agreed with whispered "Amens."

"Lord, we pray for all the changes in the lives of the ones who have been evacuated," Matt's dad prayed. "Give them wisdom to know when and if it will be safe for missionaries to return, and we especially pray for the safety of the African church leaders who remain in Zaire."

After about half an hour I heard a shuffle and saw one of the teachers whispering to Mr. Rayford. The principal nodded and tiptoed to the microphone. "Sorry to interrupt your prayers," he said, "but there's just been a phone call saying that Mr. Maxwell and Jim Temple have crossed the border safely into Uganda."

A cheer went up, and Mr. Rayford called up the choir director to lead us in some praise songs. Tears stained the faces of Rachel and Rebekah as they both cried again, but this time their tears mingled with smiles and joy at the news their father was still alive.

After the songs Mr. Rayford announced that the next day many of the Zaire missionaries would arrive at Rugendo. "We want them to feel welcome. Many of you will be sharing your homes, and we will shuffle some of the students in our dorms to make room for other families. Let's do everything we can to help and show the love of Christ during this time."

The prayer meeting ended with a few of the teachers leading in prayers of thanksgiving. Mr. Rayford praised God for his mighty power to rescue. I remembered a story from the Bible and felt like the Christians in that story who prayed for Peter's release from prison and couldn't believe it when Peter showed up knocking at the door. After the prayer meeting I walked with my mom and dad to the car. "God sure answers prayer, doesn't he, Dean?" Dad said.

"He sure does," I answered.

# CHAPTER SIX

# ESCAPE FROM ZAIRE

"Hey, Dean, look at my new catty." Matt held out his Y-shaped wooden catapult for me to see at recess the next day. It was covered with strips of black inner-tube rubber. "I asked our yard worker to make a new one for me," he said, bending down to pick up a rock. Gently putting the dove-egg-shaped stone in the soft leather pouch, he pulled the rubber straps back to his ear. He aimed high into a pepper tree and was just about to release it when a voice stopped him. "Matt Chadwick, don't you dare shoot that slingshot in the playground!"

Matt lowered his catty and turned to face Miss Arden, the first grade teacher. "You can hurt someone with a weapon like that," she said.

"But I was aiming up in the tree," Matt argued. Miss Arden stood with her hand outstretched.

"And what happens when the stone comes down?" she asked. "Give me your slingshot, and I'll let you have it back after school this afternoon," she said firmly.

Matt handed over his catty. "It's a good thing you didn't shoot," I said. "Miss Arden might have kept your catty forever."

"We should go hunting after school so I can try out that new catty on some birds," Matt said. He called Jon and Dave over, and we organized a catty hunt.

After school I ran home and dug through my underwear drawer until I found my own catty. I tossed it onto my bed. I'd never been able to get it to shoot very straight. The crotch veered slightly to the right and it affected the flight of the rocks when I shot them. As I changed into some hunting shorts, I squinted at my catty. *Maybe if I pulled the rubber straps backward and a bit to the left it would compensate for the outward bend on the right fork,* I thought. I stuck the catty into my back pocket, ran downstairs, and stuffed a few cookies into my mouth before running to meet the others.

They stood around admiring Matt's new catty, which Miss Arden had returned to Matt after school. Dave had made his own slingshot, carefully crafted with some fancy designs burned onto the handle with the wood-burning kit he'd gotten for his birthday. Jon had a metal wrist rocket from the States with brand-new surgical tubing his dad had given him.

We followed Matt into the forest that hemmed in the Rugendo Mission station. Maybe we talked too loudly, but we couldn't find any birds to shoot. The few we saw flew skittishly away.

"I give up on these stupid birds," Matt said in disgust. "Let's see whose catty can shoot the farthest." Pointing out a podo tree about fifty yards away, he said, "Who can hit that tree? If you hit it, you move back twenty paces and shoot again. We'll keep doing this until we see whose catty shoots the farthest.

"Of course," Matt said, "if you miss the tree trunk you're out of the competition because your catty has to shoot straight to be worth anything."

I looked nervously at my catty. I just had to get it to shoot straight this time.

Jon went first. His wrist rocket flung his rock straight as a bee-line, and it smacked the trunk of the big needle-leafed podo tree. Dave's catty shot his rock in a looping arc, but it also hit the tree.

Matt stood up, aimed carefully, and released. His rock sailed into the bushes past the tree trunk. "Huh? What happened?" he asked. "It had plenty of power, but I missed by ten yards. I'm going to try again."

"Your rules said if anyone missed they were out," Dave pointed out.

Matt wheeled and glared at Dave. "Well, I can change the rules if I want." He gritted his teeth, eyes flashing. I looked at Dave and Jon. None of us felt it was worth it to challenge Matt.

"Let Dean go next," Dave said, "then you can have a second try. Kind of like in high jump on field day where you get several tries at each height."

"Good rule," said Matt. "Go ahead, Dean."

Drawing a stone from my pocket, I placed it in the pouch. I held the handle of my catty in my left hand. I rotated the handle several times to calculate the best angle to make my catty shoot straight.

"Come on, Dean," Matt gruffed. "Stop messing around and shoot!"

I took a deep breath, pulled the rubber straps back past my ear, and let go. Pain stabbed my left thumb, which had been steadying the fork of the catty. I couldn't believe it! I hit my own thumb! I dropped the catty, and my knees crumpled as I knelt down and gripped my throbbing hand. Tears filled my eyes, but I was determined not to cry.

Dave knelt beside me. "Are you all right, Dean?" he asked. I nodded and let go of my thumb. It was red and already starting to swell.

"That must have really hurt," Matt said. "I'm glad you went first. I was planning to do just what you did by shifting how I held my catty to try and make it shoot straight. I guess it's not such a good idea."

I sucked my thumb and then took it out of my mouth and shook it. The pain had changed to a dull ache. "I don't think I'll shoot again," I said, standing up.

"Let me try once more," said Matt. He aimed and this time missed the tree by at least five yards. "What a useless catty," he complained. "Looks like Jon and Dave are tied for the winners. Let's go home. Maybe Dean should have Dr. Freedman look at his thumb."

I gingerly bent it and winced at the pain. "It still moves," I said. "I think it'll be OK."

We headed home. Going into my house I went to the freezer and got some ice cubes, which I put in a plastic bag. I pressed the bag against my aching thumb.

"Dean," my mom called from the living room. "Come meet our guests."

I walked in and saw Rachel and Rebekah sitting on our couch together with their parents. Smiles spread from ear to ear.

"This is Mr. and Mrs. Maxwell," my mom said. "You know their daughters from school. We went to Bible college together in Oregon before you were born. Anyway, I told Mr. Rayford that we'd like to take the Maxwells into our home."

"Hi," I said, trying to hold my injured thumb behind my back.

"What are you hiding?" my mom demanded. "Are you taking cookies again?"

"No, it's nothing, Mom," I said and retreated into the kitchen. She came and grabbed my arm.

"What happened?" she asked when she saw my purpling thumb.

"My thumb got hit by a rock," I answered. "And I put ice on it like you taught me."

"How did it get hit by a rock?" she asked.

I shrugged, too embarrassed to say I'd hammered my own thumb with my catty.

She must have decided not to make a scene because she went back to our guests. "Sit down and listen, Dean," she said. "Mr. Maxwell was just telling us how he and Jim Temple escaped from Zaire."

"Well," Mr. Maxwell said, "after we saw the soldiers' trucks coming from several miles away we knew we couldn't stay at the airstrip and wait for the plane to return. One of our Zairean friends said he knew a back road to the Uganda border. So we jumped into the Land Cruiser and drove like crazy." He shook his head. "That back road my friend knew was barely a footpath. We had to avoid stumps and holes, ditches and people's gardens. Eventually we ended up at the West Nile. We couldn't ford the Nile because it's way too deep, so we decided to abandon the car and find a canoe to take us across at night. I really didn't want to leave the Land Cruiser, but there wasn't any other way."

"I don't blame you for not wanting to leave your Land Cruiser," I interrupted. "They're great cars for driving through the bush. And they cost a lot."

"Actually, I bought this car for quite a cheap price from a Greek car dealer who seems to have a steady supply of used four-wheel drive vehicles," Mr. Maxwell answered.

"Anyway, we went looking for a canoe, and instead we found an old man with a pontoon raft he'd built from old metal petrol drums. He agreed to take us across the river and said he could carry the car as well." He patted Rebekah's knee and she grinned at him. "We stayed hidden in the woods near the riverbank until late that night waiting for the old man. When he came, we pushed the Land Cruiser onto the raft. We didn't want the sound of the engine alerting any soldiers. Once the car was on the raft we lashed it down and helped the old man paddle across."

"Did anyone shoot at you?" I asked.

Mr. Maxwell smiled. "We prayed a lot and kept our heads low, but no one shot at us. We got across safely. Our most difficult task was when we met a Uganda border patrol the next morning. They demanded to know how we'd gotten out of Zaire without proper stamps in our passports. We prayed as we waited there for hours. Finally they agreed to escort us to the nearest Uganda border post where we explained what had happened, and they stamped our passports and sent us on our way down here to Kenya. We stopped at our mission hospital near Arua and radioed that we were safe. So that's what happened. It was dangerous, but God stood by us the whole way."

His daughters gave him a big hug. "We're glad you're safe, Daddy," Rachel said.

My dad had been listening carefully to the whole story and said we needed to thank God for his wonderful protection. He paused before asking, "Why do you think used four-wheel drive cars are so cheap in Zaire?"

# THE SOCCER GAME

"I'm not sure," Mr. Maxwell answered. "I've always assumed the cars had been used for big overseas aid projects. Once a project is over—for example, building a new road or constructing a dam and putting in a hydroelectric plant—the aid group dumps all the cars at a good price to a dealer in the country who sells them cheap to people like us."

"Could be," Dad nodded. "I just had a hunch that with all the cars being stolen here in Kenya, maybe some were finding their way to places like Zaire. But you're probably right about their being used project cars."

"Mom, my neck stings." My little brother, Craig, interrupted the conversation.

"Let me look," Mom said. She pulled Craig under the light of a table lamp made from a twisted *leleshwa* tree root that we'd collected near Mt. Suswa, a dormant volcano on the floor of the Rift Valley.

"You've got a nasty rash," my mom announced. "Looks like you crushed a Nairobi eye beetle. There's really been a plague of them this year. Look, there's another one climbing up the lamp."

She pointed to the tiny orange and metallic-green bug shaped like a carrot. It causes a red, stinging rash when squished. If you scratch the rash and later rub your eyes, it causes a nasty eye infection called "Nairobi eye," which is where the beetle gets its name.

Mom took Craig to the bathroom to wash the rash with baking soda and water to stop it from spreading. The Maxwells took the opportunity to drive their daughters back up to the school and eat with them in the dining hall.

Craig giggled. "That tickles," he said.

Mom gave him a stern warning not to scratch the rash or it would spread. "Maybe I should put socks on your hands like I did with Dean when we tried to help him stop sucking his thumb."

Craig looked horrified. "Don't worry, Mom, I won't scratch my neck."

After supper I went to my room to work on my social studies report. It was supposed to be about my home state of Washington. I'd only been there once, and it didn't seem like home to me, but I got out the W–Z volume of our out-of-date *World Book Encyclopedias.* I looked up Washington State and started taking notes.

"I didn't know Washington was called the Evergreen State," I muttered to myself. "Funny, it's not green in Yakima where Grandma and Grandpa live. I remember the white snow in winter and the yellow hills in summer." After a few more minutes of reading I began to daydream about the soccer game that was set for the next day in Nairobi against the Swedish School. I would be playing center fullback, and I thought how cool it would be to run back and cover when the goalie went out of his box and have someone shoot at the goal. I'd leap to head the ball off the goal line. I finally gave up on homework and went to bed, dreams of soccer glory still spinning in my head.

The next morning my dad said he'd be in Nairobi doing some business with the national newspaper that distributed his Christian magazine across Kenya. "What time's your game?" When I told him, he said, "I'll try to stop by the Swedish School to watch," he said.

After classes we crammed into the school's Nissan van and drove an hour to the Swedish School.

"Look at their uniforms," Matt said, staring out the window of the van as we arrived. The Swedish School players were running around their soccer field, wearing new blue uniforms with yellow trim. They even had blue soccer socks with the yellow stripes just below the knees. They all wore shiny new Adidas soccer boots.

"They look as fancy as the Swedish national team that plays in the World Cup!" breathed Dave.

We looked at each other. Our team wore white T-shirts—some more tan-brown than white from the red dirt at Rugendo. We wore black shorts ordered from Haria's uniform shop in Nairobi. As we piled out of the van, we looked like a real ragtag group. Jon was the only one with real soccer socks. They were red. Some of us had soccer boots, others wore Bata tackies, which were cheap made-in-Kenya tennis shoes.

Our coach noticed us whispering and comparing outfits. "Don't worry, boys," he said. "It's not what you wear but how you play that matters. Now let's stretch out."

Even the lone scuffed-up soccer ball we used for warming up seemed to mock us. "The Swedish School has six new Adidas balls," Dave whispered to me.

By the time the game started we had almost given up. We thought a team with such cool uniforms and equipment had to be better than we were. "I hope we don't lose by more than six goals," I whispered to Dave.

The Swedish School kicked off. When their center forward started to dribble the ball, Jon darted in and stole it.

"All right, Jon!" our coach yelled. "Come on, you guys can do it!"

Jon passed the ball to Matt who faked one player and shot at the goal. The ball barely missed, going over the crossbar by inches. Their goalie hadn't even moved.

Matt clapped his hands in frustration and turned to fire up the rest of us. "We can take these guys, uniforms or not!"

A few minutes later one of the Swedish School players kicked the ball the length of the field. I trapped it and passed it to Dave in the midfield. Dave sized up his position like a chess player before laying the ball off to Jon. Jon one-touched the ball forward and Matt ran onto it, faked out the fullback, and slotted the ball into the net past the Swedish School goalie. The goalie still hadn't moved. He turned to pick the ball out of the net with his fancy lime-green goalkeeper's gloves. We were ahead 1-0!

By halftime the score was 3-0. I saw Dad on the sidelines as we drank some water. The Swedish School did better in the second half, and we couldn't get a score. Toward the end of the game they kicked the ball into our penalty box. As I prepared to trap it with my thigh, the ball hit a hardened skid mark left from a sliding tackle when the field had been wet and muddy. It bounced up and hit my hand. The whistle shrilled, and the ref gave the Swedish School a penalty kick. I felt sick.

Their best player took the penalty kick and hit the ball hard into the lower right-hand corner.

Matt patted me on the shoulder. "Don't worry," he said. "We'll make another one."

Matt's promise didn't come true. We didn't score again, but neither did the Swedish School, and we won 3-1.

After the game the Swedish School gave us juice at the pavilion at the end of the soccer field. As we drank and chatted with the Swedish School players, Matt glanced over at the parking lot. "Hey, see that Volkswagen over there?" he asked, pointing.

We looked. "It looks a lot like Brad's," I said.

"I think so, too," said Matt. He hurried over to the parking lot with the rest of us following.

Jon knelt down. "It's the right color, charcoal gray, and the right model," he said.

"Pretty beat up, too," I agreed, bending over the fender. "And look at this dent. It's in the same place as the dent on Brad's fender from the time he slipped into the ditch last rainy season."

"It's gotta be Brad's car," Matt insisted.

"Let's tell my dad," I said. "He's over there talking."

We ran over to him. "Dad, Dad," I called. "We've found Brad's bug that was stolen!"

"You what? Slow down and explain," he said.

"Brad's bug," I insisted. "It's right over here in the parking lot. Come on; we'll show you."

Dad walked with us across the parking lot. "See," I said. "It looks like Brad's bug. And look at this dent right where Brad banged his fender when he drove into the ditch."

Dad raised his eyebrows and nodded while gently scratching

his chin with his index finger. He walked around the car once, peering inside. He smiled, "Well, boys . . ."

"What are you doing with my car?" a gruff voice interrupted him. A bald white man wearing glasses with lenses as thick as the bottom of Coke bottles stood next to the Volkswagen, jingling a ring of keys in his hand.

"My boys thought it looked a lot like a car that was stolen from Rugendo recently," Dad said.

"It wasn't this car," the man stated. "I've owned this car for many years." Two of the soccer players from the Swedish School came over, and the man, who must have been their father, opened the car, and the boys jumped in the back. They looked a bit embarrassed in the beat-up Volkswagen parked next to fancy new Swedish embassy Volvos.

The man with the glasses went on. "This car of mine is very good. I don't worry about being bumped in the crazy Nairobi traffic." He pointed out the various rusting scars and dents in the car's body. "And I don't have to fear thugs with guns holding me up and stealing my car."

Dad smiled and agreed with him. He waved a friendly goodbye as the man got in and drove away.

"Dad," I chided, "you didn't ask him where he got the car. Maybe it was stolen from Brad and sold to this man. Now we won't be able to trace the thief or the dealer."

Dad shook his head. "Besides the fact that he said he's owned that VW for many years, I was about to tell you that car wasn't Brad's. It never was."

"How do you know?" I demanded.

"It had the wrong license plate, Dean. Brad's is KRY 743. This one was KRE 426."

"Couldn't they have changed the license plates?" I asked.

"Perhaps," Dad answered, "but it's a lot of risk for such an old car. I'm sure the man who just drove away in the VW is the true owner. He had no reason to lie about owning the car for years. He's the principal of the Swedish School."

That stopped my questions. After my dad left, Matt whispered, "Quick, Dean. The expiration date on the window sticker was for next August. Write it down. We need to follow up on this clue. We'll ask Brad what date his window sticker expires. If it's August, my guess is it's his car. Maybe that Swedish guy is involved some-how. I doubt the thieves could fake the window sticker."

The next day at school Jill came up to me at recess. "I heard you guys won your soccer game yesterday," she started. "Good job."

"Thanks," I mumbled.

"Have you Rhinos found any clues about who the car thieves are?" Jill asked.

"Actually, we're following up on a clue we found yesterday," I said, "but I can't discuss the details."

Jill said, "Well, we girls didn't think you Rhinos were doing a very good job. So we had a meeting yesterday afternoon and de-cided to form our own club to find out who the car thieves are."

# CHAPTER EIGHT

# GIRLS FORM CHEETAH CLUB

**"Y**ou formed your own club?" I asked, surprised. "Just girls?"

"Yes!" Jill answered. "Rachel, Rebekah, and I have started a girls' club called the Cheetahs. My little sister, Beth, is a member as well." Jill looked around and dropped her voice. "We didn't really want her, but she ran to my mom, and Mom said we had to include her."

Rachel and Rebekah sauntered over. Rebekah squinted into the sun as she looked at me. There was an arrow-shaped scar above her left eyebrow.

"Nice scar," I commented. "How'd you get it?" We Rhinos considered scars marks of honor and always had stories to tell about them.

Rebekah frowned and touched her eyebrow. "This?" she asked. "Once on a hike as Rachel pushed her way ahead of me, a branch on the path snapped back and raked me."

"It wasn't my fault, Rebekah," Rachel said. "I said I'm sorry. Besides, who cares about some old scar?" Rachel turned to Jill and grinned. "Did you tell Dean and the Rhinos that they have competition?"

Jill nodded. "I was just telling him. Anyway, Dean, our first mission is to catch the Rugendo carjackers. And we have a good clue."

"It can't be better than ours. What is it?" I asked.

"Yes, what is it?" echoed a voice from above. We all looked up and saw Freddie in the loquat tree. Freddie's real name is Fredricka Bernhardt. She speaks with a soft German accent and her parents work in Uganda. "I want to know the clue, and I want to be a member of the Cheetahs." Freddie clambered down the tree. A shoelace dangled free from her right shoe, and one sock hung rumpled, like a wounded pigeon. Her dirt-brown hair had been pulled into a ponytail and some sticks caught in it made it look like a ragged nest. She jumped the last foot to the ground and stumbled into Jill. Grabbing Jill's arm, Freddie pulled herself upright, saluted, and said, "I'm at the service of the Cheetah Club. Now what's this clue you're talking about?"

Jill looked at Rachel and Rebekah, who both shrugged. Jill smiled tightly and said, "We'll talk about membership later. I'd tell you what we're planning to do, but . . ." She turned to me. "But if I told you, Dean, you and your Rhinos would say you solved the mystery. Let's just say a friend told me about a nearby mechanic's yard that sells used car parts at a cheap price. And the Cheetahs are looking into the case."

I ran and found Matt and told him about the girls forming a club to find the carjackers before we did.

"Who does Jill think she is?" Matt demanded. "We need to investigate our clue. Do you have the window sticker dates from that Volkswagen we saw at the Swedish school?" I gave him the wrinkled sheet of paper with my scribbles. Matt squinted at it. "I can't read this," he said.

I looked. "It says August next year."

"I'll ask Brad at lunchtime what date his window sticker expires," Matt said. "We'll have an emergency meeting this afternoon at the tree house. You're the secretary, Dean. Tell Jon and Dave to be there."

I nodded. The bell rang to end recess, and I hurried back to class. I passed Freddie as she headed into the fifth grade classroom. She spit out some loquat seeds and smirked at me. I ignored her.

We Rhinos gathered at our tree house after school. Matt solemnly announced that we had two items of bad news. "First, I talked with Brad at lunch. He said his car registration window sticker expires in February. The car we saw yesterday expires in August. They don't match. So that clue looks like a dead end. I guess Dean's dad was right."

"So what's the second piece of bad news?" Jon asked.

"Jill has formed a girls' club called the Cheetahs and the girls plan to find out who has been stealing cars before we do. Dean has the details."

I told what I knew and how Jill had mentioned a roadside mechanic selling cheap spares.

"Let's go check out that new Green Victoria Garage on the road to the Makutano trading center," Matt said.

"Good idea," Jon agreed. "We can pass by the river where we first saw the stripped-down truck and see if any tracks lead from there to the Green Victoria Garage."

We hoofed it to the Rugendo River. Passing the truck skeleton, we took the path toward Makutano, a small market town at a crossroads on the main highway to Nairobi.

"See anything, Jon?" Matt asked.

Jon bent low and scanned the ground. "Nothing. The trail's too cold to expect much. There are a few footprints, but lots of people use this path to bring potatoes and bananas to the market."

Suddenly Jon held up his hand signaling us to stop. "There's something moving behind those trees," he whispered.

We crept forward and peered around the trees. "Wow, beautiful," Jon breathed.

An augur buzzard, a big hawklike bird with a white chest, black back, and a red tail, stood in the straw-yellow grass holding what looked like a baseball bat in its sharp talons.

As we got closer the buzzard blinked at us and screeched a warning. The baseball bat twitched.

"The bird has a snake!" exclaimed Matt.

"It's a puff adder," Jon added.

We stood in awe and watched as the buzzard gripped its meal until the snake stopped twitching.

"That was really cool," Matt said, as we eased away from the augur buzzard.

"I'm glad the buzzard caught that snake or we might have stepped on it," I said.

We kept going on the path to Makutano. Soon we could hear the roar of cars speeding by on the tarmac road. As we got to the main road we saw a big yellow sign with black letters warning: CAUTION Deformed Road Ahead. A massive pothole remained where heavy trucks had squished over hot tarmac, leaving a crater big enough to hide Brad's Volkswagen.

As we watched, a small Peugeot came flying down the road, ignoring the sign. The driver saw the pothole too late, and we heard his brakes squeal before the car dropped into the hole. There was a grinding crunch and a clatter and the car lurched out again. It gradually picked up speed. As it careened around a corner, something fell off and clanged into the bushes.

"He lost something," Matt said, running to the spot. "Look, here it is!" He held up a hubcap with the Peugeot lion etched on it. The driver was too far away for us to get his attention.

Matt carried our prize as we headed down the road. "We can hang this hubcap on the wall of our tree house," he said.

Ahead we saw a green board with the words "Green Victoria Garage" stenciled on it in crude white letters.

A framework of bony black-wattle poles stood in front of the garage with about twenty-five hubcaps mounted on it. A Kenyan man looked up from his work on an old Nissan minibus. He saw the hubcap in Matt's hand and asked, "Do you want to sell that? I buy and sell used hubcaps."

"No," Matt answered. "We just found this one after it fell off a Peugeot back by that pothole."

The mechanic nodded. "That's where I find most of my hubcaps. The broken up road is good for my business. Even this minibus is here because of that hole. It broke a shock absorber, and the owner brought it to me for repair."

Dave squatted and studied the broken shock absorber.

Matt asked, "What we really want to know is if you sell used spare car parts. I mean besides the hubcaps."

"I do," the mechanic answered. "And at a good price. What are you looking for?"

"Do you have any Volkswagen parts?" Matt questioned.

The mechanic frowned. "No, I don't."

"Land Rover parts?" Matt continued his questioning.

The mechanic moved back to a table under the rusty iron-sheet roof and showed us some parts.

Dave looked at his selection. "None of these could be from Jon's dad's Land Rover," he whispered into Matt's ear. "These are from really ancient Landies." Dave knew his cars, so Matt believed him.

"Why are you asking these questions?" the mechanic asked, looking serious. "You don't have a car to fix, do you? A group of girls was here earlier asking the same kind of questions. What's going on?"

"Oh, no! The Cheetahs have already been here," Matt groaned.

"I don't know what you are doing," the mechanic said. He stood straight. "I run an honest business fixing cars. And sometimes when a car is too old to fix anymore I buy it for almost nothing and take it apart and sell the used parts."

"He's telling the truth," Dave said to Matt. "We won't learn anything else here about the cars being stolen around Rugendo. We'd better head home.

"Hey, while we're here, why don't we go have a look at the *mitumba* clothes market?" *Mitumba* was a newly coined Swahili word for something that had already been used. Recently, importers had brought bales of used clothes into Kenya and on market days vendors set up stalls filled with clothes from overseas at reasonable prices.

We followed Matt as he led us to the *mitumba* market on the other side of the road. A tattered plastic sheet had been strung up over one stall that had a pile of shoes. We stopped there first. "Look at this," Jon marveled. "A pair of Nike running shoes. And it looks like they've hardly been used."

The seller noticed Jon's interest and asked, "Do you like the shoes? I can give you a very special price."

Jon knew that the key to getting a good price was to act like he didn't really want the shoes. "Oh, they're not really my size," he answered, dropping the shoes back on the pile. "Let's go," he whispered. And we moved on to another stall. This seller had an assorted array of T-shirts.

I held up a black T-shirt. "Portland Trailblazers," I said. "And look, it still has a price tag of $1.99 from Goodwill. This probably came from the same store in Portland where my parents take me to shop every time we visit our supporting churches there."

"What I really want is a pair of hunting shorts," said Matt. "That lady over there has a mountain of shorts. I'm going to dig." And he wandered away in search of some khaki shorts with big pockets and lots of zippers.

Jon decided to meander back to the shoe stall and bargain for the Nike running shoes. Dave and I stopped to buy a Farmer's Choice sausage from a man wearing a white coat and carrying warm juicy sausages in an insulated box.

"Don't forget to ask for Farmer's Choice sausages by name," Dave reminded me. We had seen in the newspaper where the company sent a mystery man called Bwana Sausage to various locations around Kenya. And if he heard you asking for Farmer's Choice sausages by name, you could win 10,000 shillings. We asked for our Farmer's Choice sausages and paid our ten shillings each, but Bwana Sausage was nowhere nearby, so we didn't win any prize.

We sat down to eat. Suddenly Dave said, "Look over there! Isn't that Jill and her Cheetahs?"

Jill saw us and came over. All the girls carried green plastic bags with the year's calendar printed on one side and an advertisement for a brand of cigarettes on the other. Little boys ran around selling the plastic bags for two shillings so people could carry their purchases.

"I see you've been shopping," I commented. "What did you buy?"

"This *mitumba* is the greatest," Rachel said enthusiastically. "I got the cutest pair of shoes, and a blouse from the Gap."

All the girls began telling us about their great bargains at the same time. Dave and I were kind of blown away by the volume. Especially by Freddie, who kept jumping in to tell her version of every story.

Matt came up carrying an identical green plastic bag. He eyed the Cheetahs warily. "Aren't you looking for car thieves?" he asked.

"We were," said Jill, "but we ran into a dead end. So we decided to go shopping. What did you buy?"

Her friendly attitude must have made Matt forget his irritation at the girls for trying to find the car thieves first. "I found some hunting shorts," he said, "and they only cost me one hundred bob."

Jon joined us. He kicked a rock along the ground ahead of him. He shook his head, "Once that guy knew I wanted the shoes, he wouldn't lower his price at all. Can you believe it? He wanted a thousand shillings!"

"Which shoes?" Jill asked. "And how much do you have to spend? I'm sure I can get them for you."

Jon and Jill plotted how she would wander past the shoe pile, look at some girl's shoes, and as an afterthought ask the price of the Nike shoes. Jon gave her three hundred shillings. We arranged to meet later outside the market.

About ten minutes later Jill arrived with shoes in hand. "I got them for two hundred," she said. Jon grabbed them, grinning. "So, are you going to give me one hundred shillings for making the bargain for you?" Jill teased.

Jon's face puckered into a frown. She laughed and handed Jon his change. I liked the sound of Jill's laugh.

"I'll buy you a Coke," Jon said. He stopped by a cart under a red and white umbrella where a young man sold ice-cold Coca-Cola. As Jon handed Jill the bottle, she murmured, "Don't turn around, but I'm certain someone is following us."

# CHAPTER NINE

# BIKE DIVING

I turned around.

"I told you not to turn," Jill hissed. "You boys keep on talking right here. I'm sure that guy is following us. We're going to hide. See if you can find out who he is." Motioning to Rachel, Rebekah, and Freddie to follow her, they slipped behind the gray cement wall of a tailoring shop. An old man sat on the veranda, his treadle sewing machine whirring as it stitched a yellow school-uniform shirt. He looked at the girls shrewdly. He nodded with his head and pointed with his chin toward a side door in his shop. The girls slipped inside.

Pretty soon a Kenyan man in greasy blue overalls strolled past. It felt like his eyes burned through us, but we kept talking and pretended to ignore him. There was a dark scar just above his left eye. As he reached the next street he looked left and right, then hurried away.

Matt called the girls out of the tailor's shop. We thanked the old man, who nodded in time with the up-and-down motion of his foot on the treadle and never said a word.

"What was that all about?" demanded Matt.

"I'm not sure," Jill answered, puzzled. "Did you find out who he was?"

"No," Matt answered. "He didn't look like he wanted to talk with us."

"I noticed him following us all around the *mitumba* market," Freddie stated. "At first I thought maybe he wanted to sell me something, but whenever I turned, he'd slide into a shadow or turn his head."

"I noticed him, too," Rachel said, "but I just thought it was my imagination."

"He followed us from the Green Victoria Garage," stated Rebekah. "I didn't want to make a big deal about it, but I'm sure he's been shadowing us since we finished asking that mechanic about car parts."

"We went to the Green Victoria Garage as well," Matt said. "The mechanic was nice at first, but when he felt we were snooping, he got angry and said you girls had already asked him a lot of questions."

"We tried not to be obvious," Jill said, "but when he asked why we needed spare parts, we didn't have a really good answer."

"I said I was German and wanted to see how well Volkswagen parts lasted on Kenyan roads," Freddie put in. "Pretty dumb answer, eh? He sent us packing after that."

"But would he really have sent someone to follow you?" Matt asked. "It's one thing to be angry when some kids come snooping, but he has nothing to hide. We looked at his car parts. No way he's selling any parts stripped from newly stolen cars. Did you see the man at all before you visited the Green Victoria?"

"No," answered Freddie. "I'm sure of it."

"Well, let's go back and ask the mechanic," Matt said.

So we walked across the street to the Green Victoria Garage. The mechanic looked up in surprise. "I thought you children had asked enough questions," he said. "I've already told you, I'm an honest mechanic."

"We believe you," Matt said, kindly, "but the girls noticed a man in blue overalls following them in the *mitumba* market. And he started following them after they left your yard. Do you know who he is?"

The mechanic's eyes widened. "I have no idea," he said, but he had fear in his eyes. I wondered what he was covering up. "No idea at all. You children should just go on back to your mission station at Rugendo where you can be safe. Please, go now."

His voice had a pleading urgency. Just then I saw our mystery man in overalls step out from the shadows behind the garage and slip away into a nearby *chai* house.

"That's the man over there!" I said. "Who is he?" I asked the mechanic.

"What man?" the mechanic replied, but I could see his eyes fixed on the *chai* house, and his fingers curled tightly over the spanner in his hand.

"You children go home like I told you," he said, turning to us. "And stop chasing after the spare parts of the cars stolen from near the mission station. They're not here. Now go!" His eyes became hard, and a scowl made his face look ugly.

We left. "Well," Matt asked as we filed down the path toward Rugendo, "do you think we're on to something?"

"The parts he had for sale certainly didn't come from any stolen cars," Dave answered, "but the mechanic did get really nervous when we asked about that man following the girls."

"We're the Cheetahs, not the girls," Freddie put in.

"Do you think you'd remember that man's face again, Jon?" Matt asked.

"I don't think I'd forget his eyes," Jon said.

"And he had a scar above his left eye," I added.

"I think the mechanic knew that man was up to no good," Jill said. "He was worried about our safety. Did you see how he told us to get back to Rugendo? Maybe the guy in the blue overalls is some kind of criminal. Whatever, I'm certain the mechanic at the Green Victoria has no ties to the stolen cars from Rugendo."

"It does look like a dead end," I said.

"Seems like it," Matt agreed.

As we passed the Rugendo River Matt paused and stared at a spot where the riverbank was about three feet higher than the muddy water. We stopped with him while the Cheetahs walked on ahead, talking and swinging their green bags full of new-to-them used clothes.

"You know what would be really fun?" Matt asked, putting his idea to words. "If we came down here with our bikes and tried riding over this ledge and into the river."

My stomach lurched. Even fast downhills scared me. But riding off into a river?

Jon jumped onto the idea. "That would be exciting!" he said.

Dave looked a little bit doubtful. "We'd have to check out the middle of the river for rocks or we could . . . ," he hesitated, not wanting to sound like a sissy. "We could, um, break our bikes on those unseen rocks if they're there," he finished.

"Sure, sure, we'll check it out for rocks," Matt said. "I'm not stupid, but all this chasing after car thieves with no success has made me bored. Let's come down after school tomorrow and give it a try."

Jon agreed enthusiastically. Dave nodded. "After checking out the bottom of the river for rocks," he said.

I tried to smile as I nodded my agreement. Inwardly I dreaded the thought of hurtling off the riverbank on my bike and plunging into the river.

The next day at recess Matt came over as we chose sides for a soccer game. "Boy, I'm so excited about jumping our bikes into the river that I can hardly listen to my teacher." He looked at me. "Are you excited, too?"

I almost told him I had a headache, or a dental appointment, or something. Matt asked, "Not scared are you?"

"Me?" I answered. "No, of course not." I tried to swallow down my fear. "I can't wait, Matt."

After school we met up at Matt's house. My blue Raleigh bicycle had a hard leather seat. My parents had bought it from a second-hand store in Nairobi and my mom had painted it herself. All the other guys had BMX bikes with some type of padding on the seat. Jon even had a new gel-seat on his bike to cushion the ride.

"Let's go," Matt said, heading his bike down the road. Ahead of Matt I saw Kamau, one of our Kenyan friends, flagging us down by waving his hand. Matt skidded to a stop, and we all pulled up next to Kamau.

"What's going on?" Dave asked. "Is your dad still in trouble about the missing *harambee* money?"

"People still blame him because the real thieves haven't been caught," said Kamau. "That makes him very discouraged and sad.

Our whole house is sad when my father is sad." Kamau paused and took a deep breath. "But that's not why I stopped you. I was asked to give you a letter." He looked behind him and then into the woods on the other side of the road. Satisfied no one was spying, he pulled out a soft grayish piece of paper that had been folded into a square and handed it to Matt.

Matt opened the note. It was written on a page torn out of a Kasuku school exercise book. Matt read out loud. "'Stop trying to find the car thieves. This is the only warning you will receive.'" Kamau looked around nervously.

"Who gave this note to you?" Matt asked.

Kamau's eyes widened. "I can't tell you," he said.

"Well," Matt said, "we'd sort of given up on finding out if someone was stealing cars and selling the spare parts, but if you tell us who gave you the note we might have a good clue as to who's stealing the cars."

"I can't tell," Kamau insisted.

"OK," Matt said, "tell the sender of the note that you gave it to us, and we understand the warning about not continuing our search for the car thieves." Kamau nodded and ran off.

"Will we really stop searching for the car thieves?" I asked.

"I didn't tell Kamau we would stop searching. Just that we understood the warning," Matt said. "We haven't found anything yet, and if Kamau won't help us, there's not much more we can do anyway. At least the Cheetahs haven't found anything either. Let's forget the car thieves and go bike diving." Matt moved off in a flurry of pedaling. His towel had started to spill out of his army-green backpack.

At the river we parked our bikes and put on our swimsuits. Dave walked into the river to check out any rocks or other dangerous objects that might lurk underwater. The river reached Dave's chest when he stood in the middle. "Mostly mud," he called, walking back and forth across the area of the river where we would splash down.

"Oops, what's this?" He bent down and his head disappeared in the swirling water until all we could see was his back. His head surfaced, and Dave spluttered as he pulled out a tree branch, black and scraggly. He threw it to us on the riverbank. "That's about it," Dave called, climbing out of the river.

"I'm first," Matt said. He mounted his bike, let out a whoop and started pedaling. As he reached the riverbank, he yanked up on the handlebars and stood up on the pedals. His bike went up in the air briefly and began to drop. Matt and his bike splashed into the river and disappeared. Soon Matt's head surfaced. "Great!" he shouted. "I'm going again." He reached down and dragged his bike, muddy and dripping, out of the river.

Jon went next, doing an almost identical jump. Then Dave drove into the river. I had to admit that the part where he floated through the air looked pretty fun. It was the landing that concerned me, especially with the hard leather seat on my bike. "Your turn, Dean," prompted Matt from behind.

"Right," I said. Taking a deep breath, I pushed off and pedaled toward the river. As my bike arced through the air I had a moment when I felt like I was flying before my fear of landing overtook me. In a panic I pushed the bike out from under me, and I made a resounding back flop in the water as the bike crashed into the river off to one side.

"Good one, Dean!" Matt cheered. "I hadn't thought of trying to jump off my bike in midair. I'm going to do that next."

We experimented with different ways to leap our bikes into the river. After my first jump I didn't have the same heart-stopping fear, and I even enjoyed diving into the river.

When we got tired, we toweled off and rode back to Rugendo. As we neared Matt's house we saw Jill, Rebekah, Rachel, and Beth. "Looks like the Cheetahs," Matt said in a mocking voice. "Find any stolen cars lately?"

"Yes!" shouted a voice from above. We looked up and saw Freddie up in a wild olive tree.

"Freddie's right. We did find a stolen car," Jill answered.

"What do you mean?" Matt asked, getting off his bike and crossing his arms in front of his chest. We all dismounted as well.

# CHAPTER TEN

# THE FISHING TRIP

"We found a stolen car today," Jill repeated.

"Whose?" Jon asked. "Our Land Rover?"

"No," Rachel answered. "Our Land Cruiser."

"When was it stolen and how did you find it?" Matt asked, not really believing the girls.

"We're not sure when it was stolen," Rebekah answered. "Sometime before we bought it."

I finally began to understand. "Did your dad buy a stolen car in Zaire?" I asked.

Rachel nodded, "After we left you at the river that day, we began talking about the *mitumba* market. Rebekah said they even call used cars that are sold in this country *mitumba* cars. We began wondering if some of the *mitumba* cars that you see for sale on the streets of Nairobi were really stolen cars. Knowing that our dad had bought his car from a *mitumba* dealer in Zaire, we asked him if our car had possibly been stolen."

"What did your dad say?" I asked. "Remember, my dad asked him why the cost of used cars was so low in Zaire."

Rachel nodded. "My dad said he doubted our car had been stolen because he had all the proper paperwork. Since Zaire is closed because of the fighting, my parents have taken a job with our mission in Nairobi so we'll be staying here in Kenya for a while. My dad got a permit for the car. He showed us the Kenyan forms where he had written down the engine number from his Zaire registration papers. I asked him if he'd ever checked to see if the engine number on the Land Cruiser matched the ones on the registration papers. He said he hadn't, so we went out to the car together and looked." She paused.

"And what did you find out?" Matt asked.

"The numbers didn't match."

Matt scratched his chin. "So you really did find a stolen car," he said. "But that doesn't solve the case of the stolen cars from here at Rugendo."

"Actually," Jill said, "we think it does help solve that case. Rachel and Rebekah's dad went to the police to report what he'd found. The police asked him to visit the head of the CID—you know, the Criminal Investigation Department in Nairobi. They've taken the name of the dealer in Zaire, and they hope this will be the link they need to break an international car-stealing ring that operates all over East and Central Africa. They think cars stolen here—"

"Like our Land Rover," Jon cut in.

"Yeah, they think cars like your Land Rover are whisked to other countries for quick sale by dealers who aren't worried about breaking laws. They're trying to trace where the Maxwell's Land Cruiser was stolen from. Anyway, they may not recover your Land Rover, Jon, but if the CID break up this carjacking ring, it's Rachel and the Cheetahs who get the credit for figuring out what was going on." She stopped.

Matt looked stunned. He couldn't answer Jill.

Jill smiled. "Face it, Matt, the Cheetahs are just smoother and smarter than you and your clumsy Rhinos."

Matt's face wrinkled in anger at that insult and he snapped, "Well, you may think you've solved the case, but we had an anonymous note today, and we know that the cars from Rugendo were stripped and sold as spare parts. And we're going to prove it!"

"We looked into the spare parts racket," Jill said. "We went and talked with that mechanic at the Green Victoria Garage, and there's nothing illegal going on there. So how are you going to prove something that's not happening?" Jill and the Cheetahs walked off.

Matt turned to us and pounded his right fist into his left hand. "We've got to solve this mystery—now!"

I explained our problem to Dad at supper. After listening carefully, he smiled and said, "Well, maybe those Cheetahs beat you on this one. It does seem that the car stealing is masterminded by some countrywide organization, and Mr. Maxwell's car gives the police a big clue in breaking up the whole thing. I don't think there's much more you Rhinos can do. The police are working on the case."

"What about Brad's VW?" I insisted. "I'm sure no carjacking gang would bother with that battered old thing. And why did we get that warning note from Kamau if we weren't close to discovering something?"

"You're right, Dean. Brad's missing car is a puzzle. It is indeed a conundrum, as my Pakistani paper dealer in Nairobi would say." He paused. "Tell you what. Why don't I take all the Rhinos trout fishing on the Thririka River on Saturday? It might heal the sting of having the girls' club beat you in your contest to find the car thieves."

"Could we go fishing?" I asked. "That would be great! And the Cheetahs haven't won yet. They've only discovered a clue."

Saturday morning, after an early breakfast of Weetabix and bananas, we picked up the other Rhinos and drove up the hill toward the Thiririka River. The river tumbled down through a steep forested valley from the high slopes of South Kinangop. Rainbow trout fingerlings had been imported years before by the British and planted in the river. Now trout, some as long as a foot, lurked in the murky pools of water where the river slowed and wound around massive trees and rocks.

Dad stopped off at the ranger post. Thick moss hung from the wooden-shingled roof. A Kenyan in a camouflage jacket and a black beret with the Kenya Wildlife Service crown on it inspected Dad's fishing license. "Remember, the Thiririka River is for fly-fishing only," he warned us.

Dad nodded. "I understand the rule. I told the boys to leave their normal fishing gear at home."

The head ranger called out to a building behind the office. A man came running over. "This is Hinga," said the head warden. "He will go with you to be sure you're safe from buffalo and elephant."

Hinga smiled, hoisted a rifle, and hopped into the back of our Land Rover. It had rained hard the night before, so my dad had to put our old Landie into four-wheel drive, and we roared and slithered up the forest road. After about twenty minutes Dad slowed down. A huge mud hole covered the road. Elephants had wallowed in the hole, leaving the mud sloppy and deep. "I'm not sure if we can make it through this bit," Dad said.

Hinga smiled. "*Hakuna matata, Bwana.* No problem," he said.

He hopped out and grabbed the *jembe,* a long-handled hoe that we carried for mud emergencies.

Hinga walked ahead, his black Bata gumboots squelching in the greasy-looking mud. Past the mud hole, Hinga stopped and motioned to my dad to drive through on the left side. Dad splashed into the mud. Halfway through the hole, the Land Rover sank and stopped. Dad dropped it into reverse and then slammed it into first gear, trying to rock the car out, but as he revved the engine the wheels only spun, splattering mud backward and digging deeper into the muck.

Hinga signaled for my dad to stop. He ran and dug with the *jembe* behind the back tires of the car. He took some cypress tree branches that had been trimmed from the trees the Forestry Department had planted for timber and threw them behind the back wheels.

"*Weka ree-vas,*" he commanded, combining Swahili and English to tell my dad to put it into reverse gear. The Landie gained traction on the branches and moved backward about a meter.

"*Haya, ngoja,*" Hinga called. "OK, wait."

He ran to the front and laid out a mat of tree branches, sort of like the people of Israel had laid out palm branches before Jesus when he rode into Jerusalem on the back of a donkey colt. Hinga swung up into the Land Rover. "*Haya, twende,*" he called. "OK, let's go."

The Land Rover bumped and crawled and gradually pulled itself out of the mud. As we picked up speed again, a terrible scraping noise came from under the car.

"Is something broken?" I asked.

Dad frowned as he stopped the car. "I hope not," he murmured as he opened the door and climbed out.

He squatted down to look under the car. "Here's the problem," he called, reaching down and pulling out one of the tree branches. He tossed it aside. "It got stuck under the rear axle," Dad said. He walked to the side of the road to wipe the mud off his hands in the wet grass.

"We're almost there." Dad climbed back into the car. Soon we stopped.

I handed my dad his fishing box. His split bamboo fly rod was wrapped in a canvas case. Dad handed the lunch basket to Matt. Jon got the small landing net. "You can carry my camera bag," my dad said to Dave.

We followed Hinga on the overgrown path that sloped sharply down to the river. Ahead trees waved. I thought it was the wind, but Hinga waved us to stop. "*Ndovu*," he announced quietly. "Elephants."

Dad whispered, "Elephants are better than buffalo. At least we know where they are and can keep out of their way. Buffalo can appear suddenly, and they attack when startled. First they gore you with their horns and then trample on you."

I studied the bush nervously, imagining a buffalo behind every tree. Hinga picked his way around the clearing where the elephants were feeding. We could hear them, but because of the thick forest we could only see vague gray parts of the elephants themselves.

Dad grabbed his camera bag from Dave and pulled out his new telephoto lens. He kept moving, trying to get a clear view of the elephants. Finally he shook his head and returned the camera to the bag. Hinga led us deeper into the valley.

As we got closer to the river we heard its soothing chuckle as it boiled over rocks and fallen logs. Tree ferns with trunks too big to span with both arms hung out in space from both banks of the river, forming a speckled canopy over the water.

At the river Dad took out his fly rod and expertly whipped the thick green fishing line and dropped his fly in a pool formed by a bend in the river. No bite. Dad tried again. Still nothing.

I hoped Matt wouldn't get bored. Dad came back to where we stood on the riverbank. "Let me have a royal coachman," he said. I opened the tackle box and gave him the colorful feathery lure he wanted.

"Wow!" Matt said when I opened the tackle box. "Those flies are cool!" He started going through the box.

Dad moved near a deep pool and motioned me over. "Here, Dean, see if you can catch a trout." He stood behind me and put his hands around me and helped me to cast. As the royal coachman settled in the water a fish broke the surface and swallowed the hook. I gave a sharp tug to set the hook. The rod bent as the trout tried to get away.

I slipped and sat down with a splash into the river. Dad laughed as I struggled to stand up and keep the fishing line taut. "You're already wet," he said, "so go after that fish."

I waded into the middle of the river as I reeled it in. I could see the trout breaking the surface in its struggle to get away.

"Throw me the landing net," Dad called. Jon tossed it to my dad, who caught it with one hand. As I pulled back with the rod, he guided the now-exhausted trout into the net.

"He's a big one!" I said.

"Supper," Dad replied, his face filled with a big smile.

I pulled out the keeper string, and we attached the fish by running the string through the fish's gill and out its mouth.

Dad let the other Rhinos try fly-fishing. He patiently untangled Matt's fly from the ferns after Matt had impetuously tried to fling it into the water.

I eyed Dad's camera bag. "Hey, Dad, can I try taking some pictures with your new telephoto lens?" I begged as the others tried to fish.

"You know I just bought that lens, Dean," he said. "It's for getting pictures of that trogan behind our house. It's a pretty elusive bird, and I want to set out fruit near a hide and get some high-quality pictures to send to *Swara*." *Swara* was a magazine focusing on Kenya's wildlife and conservation.

Dad shook his head. "No, Dean. This lens is heavy and quite expensive. I don't think you're ready yet. Besides, you're wet and muddy from falling in the river and I wouldn't want anything to happen to that lens."

I looked down at my muddy hands and sighed. I wondered if I'd ever get a chance to use Dad's new lens.

"I prefer my spinning reel," Jon announced after his failed effort with the fly rod.

"Fly-fishing is harder," Dad said, "but if you practice you can be as accurate with a fly rod as you are with your spinning reel."

We moved up the river for over an hour trying different pools, but we couldn't catch another.

Hinga told us a new settlement had been opened upriver. "The children fish the river with worms. They catch so many fish with their worms that there are not many fish left in this river."

"Let's have lunch, boys," my dad said. The sun filtered down through the canopy as we sat and ate tuna fish sandwiches with lemonade and chocolate chip cookies.

I started shivering as I hadn't yet dried out from my spill in the river. Dad put his fuzzy fishing sweater over my shoulders. "Well, boys, at least we weren't skunked." He nodded to Hinga who led us back to the car, stopping only once to show us tracks of the elusive bongo, a large forest antelope rarely seen outside of zoos.

"This is one of the best places left in Kenya for bongos," Hinga said, "but even though we see their tracks, they are very hard to spot. In my life I have only seen two."

The road had dried out a bit so we had little trouble getting back over the mud hole. Dad left Hinga at the ranger post and gave him one hundred shillings for his help. "Do you like to read?" Dad asked. Hinga nodded. Dad handed him a copy of the Christian magazine he edited.

"Where's mine?" asked the head ranger, coming over to the car. Dad gave him one as well. Hinga, who had already started reading his magazine, pointed to an open page and said, "I need to show this story to two young men who live near me." I glanced over his shoulder and saw that the story he pointed to was the testimony of a man who had been arrested for theft and had become a Christian while in prison. "Yes," Hinga repeated, "there are two men who would do well to read this story." He nodded his head and after thanking us for the magazines, he sat down in the grass and continued to read. The head ranger was so absorbed in his magazine that he forgot to say good-bye as we drove away.

Back at Rugendo we dropped off the others. At home I took out my fish to show it off to Mom and Craig. "You gut it, and I'll fry it," Mom said.

"Oh, by the way, Dean," she said, "Kamau was here for almost two hours waiting for you."

"What did he want?" I asked.

"He wouldn't tell me. He only said he needed to see you about something important."

# CHAPTER ELEVEN

# WANJOHI'S GANG DISCOVERED!

It was too late to visit Kamau that Saturday night. At church the next morning I spotted him across the aisle. I raised my eyebrows and nodded my head at him. He smiled back, knowing I'd gotten his message. We'd meet after church.

As the pastor read a greeting from one of the Psalms, a sunbird flew in the open door of the church and landed on one of the rafters. During the first prayer, the sunbird dropped down and hovered next to the vase full of cut flowers that sat on the Communion table in front of the pulpit. The sunbird dipped its slender, curved bill into the flowers in search of nectar.

After the prayer the song leader stood up and signaled for all of us to stand with him and sing the song "Sweet Hour of Prayer." As the congregation stood, the sunbird darted back up to the rafters. There he waited for lulls in the service to dive-bomb the flowers.

After church I found Kamau, and we went and stood in the shade of a wild olive tree.

"*Ni atia?*" I asked, using a Kikuyu greeting which means, "What is it?"

Kamau answered in the normal Kikuyu fashion saying, "*Gutiri na uuru,*" meaning nothing was wrong. After that, he switched to English for my sake. He knew that even though I could parrot Kikuyu greetings, I really didn't understand the language. "You remember the note I gave you?" Kamau began.

"The one that told us to stop trying to find the car thieves?" I asked.

Kamau nodded and went on. "Matt said if I told you who gave me the note you might be able to catch the car thieves. I said I couldn't tell you. I was afraid, but I knew I should tell someone because there really are some local mechanics taking apart stolen cars. I saw it myself yesterday morning when I went to Makutano to buy sugar for my mother."

"Was it the Green Victoria Garage?" I asked. "Because we went there and didn't find anything."

"No, it's not the Green Victoria Garage. It's in the backyard of someone's home. When I saw what they were doing, I knew I had to tell you. I thought you would tell your dad. He and the missionaries might do something, and no one would find out I was the one who had told." He stopped and looked down. "When you didn't come home yesterday, I got scared again and decided not to tell you. But something the pastor said in his sermon today . . . Well, I have to say what I know."

"Uh, what part of the sermon?" I asked. I was embarrassed to tell Kamau I'd been so busy watching the sunbird I hadn't listened much to the sermon.

Kamau went on. "The part where Peter wrote we should be

happy if we suffer for doing what is right. I know it's right to tell what I saw—even if it gets me in trouble."

I saw Matt with Jon and Dave and waved them over. "Kamau knows where some mechanics are taking apart stolen cars," I announced.

"Are you telling the truth?" Matt asked, his blue eyes squinting with doubt.

"Yes," Kamau answered. "Yesterday as I walked to Makutano to buy sugar for my mother I went past Wanjohi's house." He lowered his voice. "Wanjohi is the one who gave me the note telling you to stop looking for the car thieves. Wanjohi went away last year to a polytechnic school where he learned to be a mechanic. I've never seen Wanjohi working in a garage, but he says he has a good job, and he always has plenty of money. So as I passed by his house yesterday, I stopped and looked through a crack in the fence of cypress slabs that surrounds his yard. And I saw him taking apart a car."

"Can you show us where it is?" Matt asked.

"Don't you want to tell your parents?" Kamau asked.

"No," Matt said. "They might not believe us. We want to see it with our own eyes first."

Kamau looked hesitant. I think he hoped we'd turn the matter over to the adults right away so he wouldn't have to be involved or get in trouble. "Today's Sunday," Kamau said, "so they might not be working. I'll take you there tomorrow after school."

The next day we met Kamau and followed him on the path toward Makutano. After about half an hour Kamau led us into some bushes above the path. Five minutes later he motioned for us to be quiet and pointed. Below us we could see over the slab fence into a small Kikuyu compound. A house made with wood offcuts stood in the middle of the yard. It had a blue painted door. The house had a new corrugated iron roof and a gutter to collect rainwater in a new molded plastic tank. A cow stood chewing dry grass in a narrow shed. Smoke poured out of a nearby cookhouse. And in the middle of the backyard three men huddled over the engine of a pickup truck like vultures picking at a lion's kill. One of them, dressed in greasy blue overalls, stood up to stretch his back.

"That's the man who followed the girls at the *mitumba* market!" I whispered excitedly. "I can tell by the scar above his left eye."

"That's Wanjohi and his friends taking apart a car," Kamau whispered back.

"I'm sure those are the car thieves," Matt said softly. "Let's go down there and get them."

"How?" I asked.

My question stumped Matt at first. "I'm not exactly sure, but we'll think of something." He hunkered down on his haunches to think, and we gathered around him.

After a long silence, Dave ventured, "We could create a diversion."

Matt looked up. "What do you mean?"

"Remember the story in Sunday school last week about Joshua and the town of Ai?" Dave said.

Matt snorted, "Yeah, the people of Israel got defeated by a tiny town right after knocking over the walls of Jericho. I don't see what that has to do with catching these thieves."

"That was the first time Israel attacked and there was still sin in the camp. Do you remember the second time? After Achan had been killed for his sin?"

"I remember," I said. "God told Joshua to set an ambush. So Joshua obeyed and sent a large group of men to hide in ambush behind the city. Joshua and a smaller group of soldiers charged the city of Ai, then ran away as if afraid they would be defeated again. As they drew the men of Ai away from the town walls, the other men hiding in ambush rushed in and attacked the town, which had been left without anyone to defend it." I paused. "Is that what you're planning?"

Dave nodded as he rubbed his forefinger across his chin. "Something like that. Come closer and listen."

Matt smiled as he heard Dave's plan. "It should work," he said. "Yeah, I really think it could work."

Jon peered around the trees and pointed out a footpath. "That will be our escape route," he said.

We split up. Matt, Dave, and Kamau went and hid behind a wooden outhouse just outside the compound. Jon and I walked up to the gate. Taking the gate firmly in our hands, we shook it. I saw the three mechanics come out of the belly of the car and rush toward the gate.

"Run!" Jon said. We fled down the road like pellets fired out of a pip gun. We easily outdistanced the three mechanics. Before we entered the path Jon had chosen, I turned and saw Dave sneaking into the compound. Our plan was working. We sprinted down the path through the forest for about fifty yards. We dove behind a bush and listened. Sweat formed large drops that drizzled down my face. We could hear disgusted voices as the mechanics argued. The voices faded away.

"They've given up," Jon said. "Let's meet the others." We ran to a steep place where the path curls like a pig's tail. We jumped into a hiding spot below the path and waited. Within minutes we heard Matt laughing. They stopped at the curve in the path and Matt called out, "Sksss!"

Jon and I stood up. "Well," Jon demanded, "did the plan work?"

Dave held up a distributor cap. "Evidence!" he said. "The plan went perfectly. After you guys shook the gate and ran away, those three mechanics barged out after you like the Three Stooges. One slipped; another ripped his overalls on a nail that holds the gate shut. Only Wanjohi had any speed, but they lurched on after you. Dave slipped in and took this part from the disassembled engine, and we ran like the wind."

Kamau added, "We knew you'd escaped because we heard the men shouting angrily. We hid below the path until they had gone back to their yard."

"Now we can go get help from our dads and the police," Matt said. "We've got evidence."

We went to my dad's office first. "Dad, Dad," I almost shouted, "we found them, the car thieves I mean! They're working in a yard near Makutano. And we've got evidence!"

"Slow down, Dean," he said.

I caught my breath. "Now, explain again," he said. I told him about seeing the three mechanics taking apart a pickup truck. Dave showed the distributor cap.

Dad looked at all five of us. "Are you absolutely sure?" he demanded.

"Yes," we all answered.

"Let's go get the police," he said.

At the police post the officer in charge wanted us to write a report.

"There isn't time!" Matt said, slapping his hand on the ink-stained desk. Several piles of papers jumped. "The mechanics were working fast, and they'll be finished soon."

The policeman glared at Matt. "What do you know about police work?" he demanded.

Dad said gently, "I'll help you write the report when we get back, but I really do think we should hurry."

The policeman thought and nodded. "OK, let me get my gun and two other policemen." The other two men had been asleep in the nearby quarters. They stretched and yawned and then went to the clothesline to fetch their socks, hanging over the line to dry.

"Dad," I pleaded, "this is taking too long."

"I'm sorry, boys, but it's important to have the police see those carjackers and their mechanic friends in action or nothing can be done."

Finally the officer and his two men were ready. Since the police didn't have their own vehicle, they climbed into the front with my dad. Kamau climbed in the back with us Rhinos. "You're spending so much time with us, we should make you part of the Rhino club," I said.

"Good idea," Matt agreed. "We'll do that after we catch these thieves."

As we bounced along the dirt track to Makutano, Matt said, "I hope we get there in time. We're going to catch the carjackers with the evidence."

Kamau smiled. "Yes, this will show those men that they can't steal cars. They'll be caught and pay for their crimes."

"We'll show Jill and those silly Cheetahs which club is best at solving mysteries," Matt said. He pounded Kamau on the back. "Thanks to you, Kamau. I don't know how we've gotten along in the Rhino club without you."

When we arrived at Wanjohi's place the police went to the gate and knocked on it. Wanjohi opened the gate and looked surprised to see the policemen. "Is . . . is . . . is there a problem?" Wanjohi stammered.

"We have a report—well, it is not officially a written report yet—but we heard you are taking apart stolen cars," the officer said.

"Oh no, officer," Wanjohi answered. "I just fix cars. Come and see."

He swung the gate open to let us in. "The pickup's gone!" Matt hissed. In its place stood an old van used as a *matatu,* as Kenyans called the small buses that plied the roads. The *matatu*'s owner stood next to the open front door holding a broken fan belt in his hand. The front seats of the van were folded up, and a mechanic had his head inside the engine.

"Is this car stolen?" demanded the policeman.

"Of course not," said the owner. He came over and showed the policeman his logbook and registration stickers.

"Well, where is the stolen car you boys saw?" the policeman asked, turning to us.

"It was right here, it really was," said Matt. "Just an hour and a half ago. It was a green Datsun pickup, but it seems to have disappeared. The mechanics must have finished taking it apart and sent the parts away."

The policeman glared at us. "You have wasted my time. Take me home."

"They were really taking apart a car," Matt said desperately. "We even have a distributor cap from that car as evidence."

The policeman glared at the part that looked like a brown plastic cow's udder. He reached for it and examined it carefully. "This isn't an original part. It's a spare that could be purchased anywhere in Kenya. I see no evidence.

"*Twende,* let's go."

As we headed out the gate Wanjohi reached over and grabbed Kamau. "We'll get you for this," he said. Wanjohi looked up and glared at us, too. I turned back to help Kamau out of Wanjohi's clutches when I saw a black plastic sheet covering something big and bulky behind the cattle stall.

"Hey," I shouted. "What's underneath that plastic sheet?"

# CHAPTER TWELVE

# CHEETAHS SOLVE THE CASE

**T**he policemen all stopped and looked back into the yard. The officer scowled and strode over to the black plastic sheet. "Yes, tell us what's under this?" he demanded, jerking the plastic sheet up.

The plastic slipped off to reveal an old rusty tractor. It had no tires, no engine, and all the instruments like the fuel gauge had been pulled out, leaving holes like empty eye sockets in a skull. The steering wheel was cracked.

"It's just an old tractor we sometimes use for spare parts," said Wanjohi with a smirk on his face.

The police officer really got steamed when he heard this. "This trip has been *bure*," he said, emphasizing the word *bure* (pronounced BOO-ray), which means "worthless" in Swahili.

Matt whispered to me, "Boy, you really got him mad."

"I didn't mean to," I answered. "I really thought the pickup was hidden under that plastic."

"It could have been," Dave agreed as we scrambled into the back of the Land Rover.

The policemen sat stiff and silent in the front seat.

"Somehow those guys tricked us," Matt said. "I know they were dismantling a car when we first got there. They just had too much time to cover up before we arrived with the police."

Kamau looked scared. "I think I'm in big trouble with Wanjohi," he said.

"Don't worry," Matt said. "We'll see that Wanjohi is caught. Somehow!"

Back at home my mom had made tacos. She made her own soft shell tortillas. The tomatoes and lettuce came from our garden, and she had bought half a kilo of red highland cheese from the Njoro Valley cheese factory to go on top of the meat.

Just as we started to eat, the electricity went off. "There go the lights again," my mom complained. "That's the third evening this week. I think the Kenya Power and Light Company should change its name to Kenya Power and Darkness."

We laughed at Mom's joke. She didn't. She lit a candle as Dad fumbled with the pressure lantern. I held a flashlight while he poured some purple methylated spirits into the kidney-shaped metal starter reservoir. He lit the spirits, which burned hotly. The flames leaped up until the lamp's mantle began to glow.

Dad pumped the red-knobbed handle before turning the lantern on. The mantle puffed out with a loud hiss and gave off a brilliant white light.

"There we go." Dad set the lamp on the table. As we finished eating he leaned over and stared closely at the base of the lamp. It was made of shiny stainless steel and curved like a convex mirror. Dad put his nose less than an inch away from the lamp base and stuck his tongue out.

Craig and I burst out laughing at the distorted image of Dad's face reflected in the lamp. "Is that really what you look like, Daddy?" asked Craig.

"Try it," Dad said, urging Craig closer. "Make a face, but be careful not to burn yourself."

Craig put his face next to the lamp base, stuck a finger in one nostril, and pulled it sideways. Dad laughed harder than I did, but Mom was not impressed. "That's so childish," she said, still irritated by the power cut.

I showed my profile and pulled on my ear. Craig and I giggled. Dad stood behind Mom. "Come on, honey," he said. "Give it a try."

At first Mom refused, but finally she put her face next to the lamp base and stuck out her tongue. Her ridiculous reflection was too much. She cracked up laughing as well.

After supper my mother said I wouldn't have to do the dishes since it was dark. Just then the electricity came back on. "Do I have to do the dishes now?" I asked. "You just said I didn't have to."

"Well," Mom said, "that was because the electricity was off. But now that it's back on . . ."

"Please, Mom," I pleaded.

She smiled. "I said you wouldn't have to do the dishes, so I'll keep that promise." I thanked her and went to my room to do some more research about the history of the Yakima Indians for my report on Washington State.

The next day I met Jill on the way to school. "Did you see the *Nation* newspaper this morning?" she asked.

"No." My dad had his copy of the paper delivered directly to his office.

"There's a big article on the front page," Jill said. "It tells how the CID arrested about twenty people involved in a carjacking and smuggling ring. There was even a picture of twenty-five cars that were confiscated in Zambia. Twenty-four of them came from Kenya—Mercedes, Land Cruisers, BMWs, Pajeros, all kinds of expensive cars. They caught the thieves before they had a chance to change registrations and sell them in Zambia."

"Sounds like the police did a good job," I agreed.

"The article said the organization had been operating in most of East and Central Africa. Through united efforts of police departments in several of the countries, the car stealing and smuggling ring has been broken up." She paused. "So we solved the case."

"Just because the police caught some car smugglers doesn't mean you're the ones who solved the case," I answered. "Anyway, those cars they rounded up were in Zambia, not Zaire. So I don't see how you can claim to have solved the mystery."

"We did," Jill answered. "The article mentioned that the first big break in the case came when a missionary from Zaire reported to the CID that a car he'd bought in Zaire was stolen property."

I scratched my head. "Did the article really mention a missionary from Zaire? Did it name Mr. Maxwell?"

"No, but it said the police started their investigation with that used car dealer, and they traced the robberies and sales of the stolen cars to various import/export companies that forged papers and sold the cars in different countries. In fact, the article said some of the cars stolen in Tanzania and Malawi were later sold in Kenya. Anyway, now they've caught the ringleaders and the articles says they hope the armed carjackings will drop off."

We met Matt right below the school. "And it's all thanks to the Cheetahs and our sleuthing skills!" she ended.

"What's she talking about?" Matt asked. I explained and Jill filled in the details. As she spoke, the Maxwell sisters came over and listened. Rachel corrected Jill a couple of times. When they finished, the girls looked smug.

Matt looked stunned. "You girls did a good job," he said grudgingly.

"A real good job!" a shrill voice called down from a nearby tree. I looked up. Two denim-covered knees gripped the trunk of the tree while Freddie smiled down at us. "Cheetahs are the best," she said.

Matt whirled and walked toward the drinking fountain. He grabbed my shoulder, pulled my head next to his, and hissed, "Dean, pass the word that we Rhinos have an emergency meeting at the clubhouse after school! And can you bring Kamau, too?"

At our tree house, Kamau gripped the ladder tightly as he climbed up. "This treehouse is wonderful," he said. He looked out the window but quickly closed his eyes and sat down.

Matt unfolded a copy of the *Nation* newspaper he'd gotten from his dad. "See these pictures?" he ranted, banging on them with the back of his hand. "They are evidence that the Cheetahs solved the mystery of the armed carjackers."

"That's not a bad thing," Jon answered. "My dad says there's a chance our Land Rover may be recovered."

"It's not all bad," Matt agreed. "I do hope your car is found, but there's something here that really stinks! The Cheetahs played a big part in solving the mystery, and they're just a bunch of girls. We have to get even!"

"How?" I asked.

"By solving the mystery at Wanjohi's garage," he answered. "Didn't we see them dismantling a car to sell it as spare parts?"

We looked at each other. "I think so," Dave said, "but we could have made a mistake. Maybe those mechanics were just fixing that pickup. And it seems the mystery of the stolen cars has been solved. Maybe we should just congratulate the girls and forget about stolen cars."

Kamau looked down. "I don't want to go back to Wanjohi's garage."

"But the disappearance of Brad's Volkswagen still doesn't fit in with the stolen car smuggling ring. All those other cars are almost new," I put in.

"I've got it!" Jon interrupted.

"What?" Matt asked.

"Why didn't I catch on at first?" Jon chided himself.

"What?" demanded Matt again.

"At Wanjohi's yard yesterday. Did you notice the truck tire tracks?" Jon asked.

We shook our heads.

"How stupid of me not to recognize what they meant."

"Tell us," Matt commanded. He looked ready to strangle Jon.

"We saw them dismantling a pickup truck, right?" Jon asked.

"Right," Matt answered.

"When we came back later we saw them working on an old *matatu* van."

We nodded.

"So what vehicle made the large tire tracks? Remember the mud puddle just in front of Wanjohi's gate? When we went with the police there were big truck tire tracks. The kind where the back end of the truck has two wheels on each side. I know those truck tire tracks weren't there when we first looked over the fence into Wanjohi's yard."

"You could be right," Dave joined in. "The mechanics had taken apart almost everything by the time we saw them. Even the fenders had been removed."

"I'm sure they got a bit worried that we'd seen something," I said. "So I'll bet as soon as we ran away, they took all the parts, including the chassis, and put them into a big truck and drove away. Maybe they have some central storehouse where they package and sell the used parts."

"Well, it seems there are still some more car thieves to be caught," Matt said. "We'll show those Cheetahs. Now, what should we do?"

Kamau shook his head. "I don't think the police want to hear about our discovery after our last visit with them to Wanjohi's yard."

"You're right," Matt said. "We're going to have to prove these guys are stealing cars, taking them apart, and whisking the parts away. We're going to have to catch the mechanics in the act of taking apart a stolen car."

"I think I know a way we can trap them," I said.

# CHAPTER THIRTEEN

# THE RHINOS SET A TRAP

Everyone turned and looked at me, surprised that I had a plan. Usually I just followed Matt's directions. I wasn't used to leading. At first I couldn't speak. Matt demanded, "Well, Dean, you've gotten our attention. What's your great idea for a trap?"

"Well," I began, "the hard thing is getting the police to come to Wanjohi's at exactly the right time to catch them in the act. And unless the police have real evidence, it's our word against the guys at Wanjohi's. Right?"

"Brilliant observation," Matt answered, with a bite in his voice. "What's your point, Dean, and what's your trap?"

"If we could go back to the place you showed us, Kamau, that looks down over Wanjohi's yard, we could wait until we actually saw the mechanics taking a car apart."

"That's what we did last time," Matt said. "And it didn't work because it took the police too long to come."

"That's where my plan starts," I went on. "If we took a camera with a telephoto lens, we could take pictures of Wanjohi and his friends. And by showing the pictures to the police as evidence they'd be able to take action."

The scowl on Matt's face disappeared. "Hey, Dean, that's not a bad idea, but where will we get a camera with a telephoto lens?"

"I'm sure my dad would let us use his," I answered with more confidence than I felt. Dad's Nikon camera was his most prized possession. I wasn't at all sure he'd let us Rhinos use his camera or his telephoto lens. He hadn't even allowed me to take a picture with it on our fishing trip. I didn't want to ask and be told no after I'd promised the other Rhinos we could use it, but there was no danger of getting it wet and muddy on the hill behind Wanjohi's house.

"Sounds like a good plan," Matt said. "Let's meet after school tomorrow with the camera and go hide above Wanjohi's and take the pictures."

I ran home the next day after school and went into my father's room. He had left his leather camera bag next to his desk. I opened the bag. Dad's Nikon lay snuggled in a camera-shaped hole in black velvet-looking material. Several lenses lay in slots next to the camera. The telephoto lens gleamed like a piece of black obsidian, the volcanic glass that littered the hills around Rugendo. I took a deep breath. It would be easier not to ask permission. I told myself that as long as I didn't break it, it wouldn't be wrong.

Looking over my shoulder to be sure no one saw me, I lifted the lens out of the bag. I took out the camera and checked to see if it had film in it. I attached the long lens just as my father had shown me on a recent trip to a game park.

*What if someone sees me carrying this?* I thought. I set the camera down and got my school backpack. I dumped my books and homework on my bed. Odd pieces of broken pencils, lint, and Big G bubble gum wrappers fell out with the books. I hurried back to

my dad's room, put the camera in the backpack, and zipped it up.
As I stepped out of my parents' room I heard the outside door
open.

My heart flopped like the big toad that had gotten stuck in our
bathtub the week before.

"Hi, Dean. How was school?" Mom asked as she walked in the
door.

"Uh, fine," I said, shifting the backpack and feeling sure she
could see the shape of the camera.

"I'm on my way to a women's Bible study, and I stopped by the
house to get my Bible," Mom said. "Help yourself to some cookies. They're on the counter. You look hungry."

I was glad she mistook my nervousness for hunger. "Thanks." I
grabbed a handful of cookies and headed for Matt's house.

The others were waiting for me. "Do you have the camera,
Dean?" Matt asked.

I nodded. "Has anyone seen Kamau?"

"No," Matt answered. "We can't wait forever or there won't be
enough light to take the pictures. He knows where we're going.
He can catch up to us." We headed off the path to Makutano.

As we got near Wanjohi's place Matt let Jon lead the way so we
wouldn't be seen. Jon picked a path through the bushes as lightly
as a bushbuck. Soon we were in position above Wanjohi's house,
but we couldn't see any mechanics or any cars in the yard.

"We've failed again," Matt said. "No one is here."

"Just wait," Dave said. "No one said this would be quick and
easy. Haven't you ever watched those American cop shows where
they sit for hours in an unmarked car waiting for something to
happen?"

"I hate waiting." Matt fidgeted with his belt buckle. "Maybe I'll go home and let you guys take the pictures."

"But then we'd get all the credit for catching the thieves," Dave pointed out.

That thought hit Matt hard. "Yeah, we'd better all stick together," he said.

We sat and waited. A metallic-blue fly buzzed and settled on my nose. I waved my hand in front of my face to chase it away.

"I hate bluebottles," Jon said, swatting at the fly which now buzzed around his head. "My dad told me how they land on your food and suck bits of food into their mouths. They spit it back out on your food and suck it up again. He says a lot of diseases are passed on because of these flies. They're always landing in cow dung and stuff like that before they get on your food."

"Stop!" Matt ordered. "It's bad enough sitting here waiting without you telling me gross facts about bluebottle flies."

A distant boom interrupted Matt. Clouds the color of a wildebeest boiled up over the ridge above us. "Looks like a storm is coming," Dave announced.

"What if these guys don't take a car apart today?" Matt asked. "This plan won't work."

"You're right," I answered. I didn't know what I'd tell Dad if he found out I'd borrowed his camera. If the camera got wet and ruined, I didn't think he'd ever forgive me. My plan was turning into a disaster.

Thunder growled again followed this time by two electric flashes of lightning. The first large drops of rain fell, and we could hear the dull roar as the rain arrived, pelting the forest leaves as it neared us. I shoved the camera into my backpack on my lap. I hunched over to cover the backpack so the camera wouldn't get wet.

"We might as well go home," I said. "I can't take any pictures in the rain without ruining my dad's camera." Another thunder crash vibrated the trees where we hid. Rain drooled down the tree trunks and spattered off the leaves, but the tree cover kept us from getting completely soaked.

"You're right, we should head home," Matt agreed, "but we'd better wait until the rain slows down a bit."

We huddled down to wait out the storm. Jon saw it first. "Someone's moving down in Wanjohi's yard," he informed us in an excited whisper.

Dave stood up to see what Jon was talking about. "It's Kamau," Dave whispered to us. We all stood up to watch.

Kamau dodged to the left, but Wanjohi and someone else in greasy blue coveralls grabbed him by the neck of his T-shirt and dragged him like a disobedient goat on a rope. They shoved him under the shelter of the overhanging iron roof. Wanjohi slapped Kamau in the face and Kamau fell to his knees in the mud.

"Let's rescue Kamau," I said and stood up.

Matt tugged on my arm. "In a minute, Dean. We won't help by running down now. It's most likely they're punishing him for leading us to this place. Remember Wanjohi's warning after we came here with the police. If they see us here again, they'll probably do something even worse to Kamau."

The other man kicked Kamau in the rear end, and Kamau fell headfirst into a mud puddle. They shouted something, but we couldn't hear it over the sound of the rain. Kamau stood up and stumbled toward the gate. Wanjohi and his friends laughed at him.

As Kamau limped away I kept looking at Wanjohi's yard. Wanjohi stood by the door of his house talking with his friend. Wanjohi stuck his index finger into his ear and moved it furiously up and down to scratch some deep, inside itch. He turned and spit into the mud puddle before stepping into the wood-slab house and shutting the door.

"Wanjohi's gone in. It's safe to run after Kamau now," I reported. Jon had already started down the hill with Matt on his heels. The rain had tapered off to a light drizzle. I ran clumsily, bent over my backpack to protect the camera.

We soon caught up with Kamau. "Are you OK?" Matt asked.

"I'm fine," Kamau answered. He tried not to limp. "Why do you ask?" He looked away and kept walking.

"We saw what happened back at Wanjohi's," Matt said. "Why did they slap you and kick you?"

Kamau's eyes filled with tears, but he blinked them back. "I was on the way to meet you when Wanjohi came from behind a tree and said I was to blame for bringing the police. I told them they were to blame because they stole cars."

I thought of the camera in my backpack. *I didn't really steal it,* I said to myself. *I just borrowed it.*

"They dragged me here and beat me up so I would be too afraid to try to stop them."

"We're sorry," Matt said. "We're the ones who got you into this mess."

"It's all right," Kamau answered. "My heart feels good. I did the right thing. And like the Bible says, it is a good thing when we suffer for doing right. I just wish the police had caught them. Then they wouldn't keep threatening me."

"We didn't get any pictures," I said. "They weren't taking apart any cars."

"The plan will work," Kamau said. "As I walked away I heard them say it was a good thing I was out of the way because their friends were planning to steal a car tonight, and they'd have to work hard tomorrow."

"We can come back tomorrow and get the pictures we need!" Matt said.

I nodded, feeling a little hollow. I'd been plotting some way to slip the camera back so my dad would never know I'd taken it. Now I'd have to figure a way to borrow it again! I put on a sickly smile and said, "Sure, great. We'll try again tomorrow."

At home I heard Dad talking to Mom. I couldn't get into their bedroom to return the camera, so I hid it under my bed. Pangs of guilt gripped my stomach.

At supper Dad asked me about my day. I told him it had been great. As the meal went on I relaxed. Dad hadn't noticed his camera was gone. If I was lucky, he wouldn't need it the next day, and I could leave it under my bed and take it in the afternoon when we returned to Wanjohi's place to get the pictures we needed. Part of my heart stayed frozen with fear and I wondered if Wanjohi and his friends felt the same way I did while they hid a stolen car at their place.

The next morning as I walked down the stairs to breakfast I heard Dad shout from his bedroom, "Hey! Someone stole my camera!"

# CAUGHT IN THE ACT

**D**ad strode across the living room carrying his empty camera bag. "Look," he called to my mom. "Someone took my Nikon and the new telephoto lens." The camera-shaped form in his camera bag was empty. Anger flashed in Dad's eyes.

"First it's cars, now thieves are breaking in and stealing cameras," he ranted.

"There's nothing to show anyone broke into the house," my mother said, trying to soothe him.

"Then it's an inside job," Dad said. "We'll have to ask Mary, our house help, when she gets here."

"It can't be Mary," my mom pleaded. "She's been faithful for years. Nothing's ever gone missing since she's worked for us. She even gives me the shilling coins that fall out of your pockets when she does the laundry. It can't be Mary. She's like part of the family."

Dad grudgingly agreed. "You're right, but maybe someone came to visit her yesterday and slipped in and took the camera." He began pacing again. "I can't believe it! How can my camera be stolen? And why today? This is the day I have an interview with the church bishop about how the church is planning to organize special homes for AIDS orphans."

Every word from Dad's mouth seemed to pound a nail deep into my heart. I wanted to tell him I had his camera, but he looked so angry. I leaned back against the wall and shivered a little.

Dad looked at me sharply. "My camera's gone, Dean," he said. "Can you believe the nerve of some thief coming right into our house and stealing my camera?"

My stomach churned with fear, but I knew what I had to do. "I think I may know where your camera is," I began. I looked down at my battered tennis shoes.

Dad came and leaned down over me. I could smell he hadn't brushed his teeth yet this morning.

"What are you talking about, Dean?" he asked.

"Your camera is upstairs under my bed," I said, starting to cry. I couldn't say any more.

Dad took me to the couch and sat me down. "Stop crying, Dean, and tell me why my camera is under your bed." He wasn't as angry as I'd expected, but he wasn't happy either.

"I took it yesterday," I admitted. I bit my lower lip. "And I'm really sorry—"

"You took it!" Dad cut me off. "Why? Don't you know taking something without permission is stealing? I'm glad you're sorry, but you know that's my special camera. Why did you take it without asking me? And why the new telephoto lens?"

"We thought we could snap pictures of the mechanics when they were taking apart stolen cars and persuade the police to arrest Wanjohi and his gang."

"You what?" Dad began in angry amazement. He paused to get

himself under control. "The car-stealing ring was broken up a few days ago, remember? And when we brought the police to check on those mechanics the other day, there was no sign of them taking apart stolen cars. It looked like they did an honest business as mechanics fixing broken-down cars. I was right there with you. I don't understand why you're still trying to pin something on those mechanics."

I bit my lower lip. "I thought I could just borrow it and give you the film to develop for us after we took the pictures. I figured when you saw the pictures, you'd know I borrowed the camera for a good purpose."

"Maybe you and your Rhino friends can't handle the fact that some girls helped catch an international gang of carjackers. Now you're grasping at straws to show you can still solve mysteries. You say you borrowed my camera, but when you borrow without asking, it's the same as stealing."

I waited for Dad to cool off, then ventured, "The Rhinos think the mechanics tricked us when we brought the police. So we decided to keep watch on the mechanics. I took the camera to get pictures of them dismantling cars."

"And did you catch them in the act this time?" Dad asked.

"No," I admitted, "but we saw Wanjohi beating up Kamau."

Dad folded his arms across his chest. "That doesn't seem like the actions of innocent mechanics," he said. "Maybe you guys are on to something."

Encouraged, I went on, "Kamau said the mechanics would have a new car to take apart today. I would have put your camera back, but I knew I needed it again today."

Dad sat back. "Dean, taking the camera without asking me was wrong. I'm going to have to punish you for that." He rubbed his unshaven chin. "But," he went on, "it does seem you Rhinos really have stumbled onto a second, separate gang of car thieves that uses Wanjohi's yard to take the cars apart before selling them as spare parts." He looked at me. "What's your favorite possession?"

I wasn't sure whether it was my air rifle or my bike. Finally I said, "My air rifle."

"Go get it," my dad said. "I'll keep it for a week as your punishment for taking my favorite possession without asking. And bring my camera as well."

I brought him his camera and my rifle. He checked out his camera, which hadn't suffered any damage in the rain. "I'm very glad to get this back," he said softly. He put my rifle in his closet behind a wire coat hanger loaded with old neckties. "You can have your gun back next week." He put his arm around me, and we walked to the kitchen table for breakfast.

"I really am sorry, Dad," I said. "I felt so guilty the whole time I had the camera. I kept telling myself I really hadn't stolen it."

"Psalm 32 says that when we hide our sin it's like our bones are melting, or like we're sweating it out in the noonday sun," he said. "When you told yourself you were borrowing my camera, you were hiding your sin."

"You're right," I said. "I felt terrible the whole time, wondering if you'd find out. Now that you know I stole your camera, I feel relieved, even though you've taken my air rifle for a week."

We sat down on the couch and prayed together. "God, forgive me for stealing Dad's camera," I prayed.

Dad confessed his anger at me for stealing the camera and thanked God for his forgiveness.

After giving me a hug, he asked, "So what time were you Rhinos planning to go to Wanjohi's to take pictures?"

"We were going right after school, but we probably won't go now that we don't have a camera."

"My interview and photo session with the Bishop is set for this morning. I can be back by four o'clock. If you get the Rhinos here after school, I'll go with you and take the pictures we'll need to get the police to take action."

"You will? Oh, Dad, that's great." He gave me a big bear hug.

That afternoon my dad was home waiting for me. "How was your interview with the bishop?" I asked, dropping my books on the steps leading to my upstairs bedroom.

"Very good. It's very encouraging to see the church doing what Jesus called us to do and reaching out and helping the helpless," Dad answered. He set down his cup of coffee and reached for his camera. He flicked open the back, removed his film of the bishop, and popped in a new roll.

"I'm ready," he announced. "Let's go take some pictures of these car thieves."

The other Rhinos arrived at our house. "We'll go by foot," my dad said, "so we don't scare the mechanics away." Having said that, he let Matt and Jon lead the way.

We passed by Kamau's house. Matt called and Kamau came out. "Are you ready to go with us?" Matt asked. Kamau nodded. He looked relieved to see my dad.

As we walked, Matt questioned Kamau. "Are you sure you heard Wanjohi say they'd take apart a car today?"

Kamau hesitated. "They said they'd have to be ready since their friends planned to steal a car last night, but as with any plan, it's always possible the others failed to steal a car."

113

"All we can do is go and see," my dad said. We hiked up the path.

As we neared Wanjohi's we stopped talking and walked as quietly as we could. We gathered on the hill above Wanjohi's yard where we could see the mechanics hovering around a white Toyota Corolla. The hood was up like a hippo's upper jaw when it yawns, and two men were taking apart the engine while Wanjohi dismantled large body parts like doors and fenders.

"You boys were right," Dad whispered. He focused his camera and began clicking. After several minutes he stopped and looked around. "I want to take pictures from higher up to get a better angle. Help me climb that tree." We gave him a shove as he jammed his foot into the crotch of a pencil-cedar. As he pushed off from there he slipped and fell backward, twisting his ankle. He hit the ground with his back and made a hollow thumping sound. The camera made a soft landing on Dad's growing middle-aged tummy.

"Are you OK, Dad?" I asked.

He grimaced as he tried to stand up and put his weight on his ankle. His face twitched in pain. "I think I've sprained my ankle, boys." He hobbled over and sat down in the grass and began massaging his already-swelling ankle. "I'm sure it will be all right," he muttered. He looked at me. "Dean," he asked, "can you climb the tree and get the rest of the pictures we need. Try to zoom in on the faces of the mechanics." He explained how to use the camera in detail in case I'd forgotten what he had taught me in the game park.

I nodded as I listened. I slung the camera around my neck and climbed the tree. I wedged myself against the trunk and used a branch to support the heavy telephoto lens and started taking pictures. I got several close-ups of Wanjohi's face as he pulled a door off its hinges. I kept on focusing and clicking until the camera began to beep at me.

"Film's finished," I whispered. Dad nodded and pulled out another roll and threw it to Matt who tossed it up to me. I rewound the film in the camera and put in the new roll. This time I zoomed in and took several pictures of the license plate of the car. After another ten minutes of picture taking I'd finished the second roll as well.

"I think that will be enough," Dad said. I climbed down. Kamau had fashioned a walking stick for my dad who winced and hobbled back down the hill with us to Rugendo.

"We really caught the thieves in the act," Matt said. "We'll show those Cheetahs how to catch car thieves."

At home Dad put some ice on his ankle. Mom wanted him to get an x-ray, but Dad refused. "I've played enough sports in my day to know a sprain from a broken bone."

After supper he asked if I would go down with him to his darkroom to develop the pictures. I was thrilled at the chance. He grunted in pain with every step and decided we'd better drive down to the office. We entered the darkroom. Dad shut the door and told me, "Pull the heavy black curtain across to block any light coming in the cracks around the doorframe." He set out the canisters of film, the developing chemicals, and the plastic developing containers before switching off the light. The room went completely black. I could hear him popping open the film canisters and threading the film into the developing cans. "How can you do that in the dark?" I asked.

"I close my eyes," Dad said. "It's always easier to feel in the dark if you close your eyes. When your eyes are open, even in complete blackness, your brain tries frantically to gain vision through the eyes. But if you close your eyes, the brain knows it can't see, and your other senses become stronger. Especially the sense of touch."

I closed my eyes, but everything still felt and seemed dark to me. "There, the film's all inside the developing cans," Dad said, flipping on the red safelight.

Dad poured some developer chemicals into the plastic container. "Take this and agitate it," he said. He touched my shoulder and passed the container to me. The container had sides that were made of a soft, rubbery kind of plastic, and I squeezed the sides and shook the containers so the developer would touch all the film evenly.

"That's long enough," said Dad after about five minutes. He took the container back and poured the developer down the sink. He let some clean water flow into the container as a rinse before dumping out the water and pouring in another chemical called the fixer, which stopped the film from developing any further.

When at last the film was finished, Dad took it out of the container and held the still-dripping negatives up to the light. "Let's see what we have," he said.

# CARJACKERS ARRESTED

I waited as Dad examined the negatives. He didn't say anything. Had my pictures been out of focus? Worse, had I failed to roll the film in properly? Had we gotten any photographic evidence of the car thieves at work?

"Is anything wrong?" I asked.

"Nothing," Dad answered, whistling through his teeth. "Your pictures taken from up in the tree are excellent—even better than the pictures I took!"

I crowded near him and could see the eerie reversed images on the ghostly black-and-white film negatives. I could see Wanjohi's face clearly—only it was a white face since the images on a film negative are backward.

Dad clipped the film negatives to a clothesline strung across one side of the darkroom. "I'll let these dry overnight," he said. He clipped a weight to the bottom of the strips of film to keep them from curling up. "Tomorrow I'll make prints first thing and take them to the police. Then . . . aaah!" He leaned heavily against the counter.

"What's wrong?" I asked.

"My ankle really hurts," he said.

At school the next day I told the other Rhinos how my dad said my pictures had been even better than his. "What are you boys whispering about?" Jill asked as she and the Cheetahs walked by.

"You'll find out later," Matt answered, using remarkable self-control not to brag about how close we were to catching another group of car thieves.

After school I went to my dad's office. I was surprised to see him sitting back with a large white cast on his foot and two aluminum crutches next to his desk.

"What happened?" I asked.

"The police caught the carjackers!" Dad answered.

"I was asking about your foot," I said. I stopped as I realized what Dad had said. "Do you mean they caught the thieves? Really? Wanjohi and his friends?"

Dad nodded and explained how he'd printed the pictures showing Wanjohi and his crew of mechanics in action. "I brought them to the police and the officer got very annoyed that Wanjohi had tricked us on our first visit. The police marched right up and arrested Wanjohi and the other mechanics."

"All right!" I interrupted. "My plan worked!"

"Yes, and I heard they had a confession within an hour and names of the men who did the actual carjacking. They arrested six men from Makutano and confiscated some weapons as well. Including the pistol that Dr. Freedman has identified as the one used to hold him up and steal his new Land Rover."

"How did Dr. Freedman recognize the pistol?" I asked.

"He used to be in the army so he knows weapons. Anyway, they've all been arrested and put in remand where they'll wait for a trial. The evidence against them is strong. Especially your pictures, Dean."

"And your foot?" I asked, pointing rather foolishly at the cast and crutches.

Dad shook his head. "It kept hurting, so I had Dr. Freedman take an x-ray. It showed a break in one of the bones, so I've got a cast and these." He grabbed his crutches and pretended to use them like guns. "Rugendo Rhinos hold up carjackers," he said. "That would make a good headline for the newspaper."

"Sorry about your foot, Dad, but I can't wait to tell the guys that we helped catch the carjackers." I ran out to find the others.

When Matt heard what had happened, he was so excited that he led the Rhinos to Jill's house.

"Hey, Jill, we have news for you Cheetahs," Matt called. I could see the girls on the porch. "Guess what?"

"Still searching for carjackers, Matt?" Jill asked. Freddie laughed hysterically, while Rachel and Rebekah just smiled.

"No need to keep searching," Matt said. "We found them. Dean took pictures of them and now they're in jail."

"What are you talking about?" Jill demanded.

"Dean, you explain," Matt ordered.

I did and when I finished, I said, "So you Cheetahs helped the police identify an international gang of car thieves and smugglers, while we caught another gang who were hijacking cars around here and selling their parts."

Jill thought for a moment, then turned her back and began whispering with the others. After some silence, Jill turned and announced, "So I guess that makes it a tie. We each solved a mystery that led to carjackers being caught. Congratulations,

Rhinos." With that she and the Cheetahs turned and went into the house.

As we walked away Matt punched me in the arm. "Why did you have to explain it that way?" he demanded. "Now the girls think they're as good at solving mysteries as we are."

"Sorry, Matt," was all I could mumble. The way Jill had claimed a tie had squelched our triumph at catching Wanjohi's gang. We split up, and I headed home.

That night Brad had dinner at our house. My mom insisted he eat with us a few times a week to get a decent meal. She was afraid he would starve to death on his bachelor's diet of peanut butter and plum jam sandwiches. Dad told him all about my photos, which helped the police round up a local gang of carjackers.

Brad commented, "I guess my old VW bug was stolen and sold as spare parts."

I still didn't think anyone would want the parts of his old car, but we had no other way to explain what had happened to his Volkswagen.

As I waited for a bath after supper—Mom had let my little brother, Craig, go first—I picked up a copy of the *Nation* newspaper. Inside was a story telling how a politician's house had been robbed, and the thugs used the man's Mercedes Benz to make a getaway. Later they abandoned the car in a nearby forest where the police found it and took it to the police station.

"I wonder," I thought. "Brad's car disappeared the night the *harambee* money disappeared."

The next day I told Matt about the article I'd read and my suspicions. "Maybe whoever stole the *harambee* money used Brad's car as a getaway vehicle and abandoned it. Brad always left his car unlocked, so it would have been easy for anyone to hot-wire it."

"You might be onto something, Dean, but where would we start looking?"

"Well, Brad's bug is not at our local police post. I thought we could ride our bikes up to the district police headquarters at Mutitu next Saturday. It's the biggest police station around. And, to be honest, I don't think Brad's car would have gotten very far."

"Why don't we go tell Kamau what we're thinking," Matt suggested.

We saw Kamau's father sitting on a stool outside his house. "Kamau's down by the river with some of our sheep," he said.

We found Kamau. "Your dad didn't look very happy," I commented over the bleating of the sheep.

"He still thinks people blame him for the stolen *harambee* money," Kamau stated. "We all feel ashamed."

He brightened when we told him our theory that Brad's car might have been used as a getaway vehicle by the real *harambee* thieves. "I hope you're right," Kamau said, "but let's not tell my father until we find out if it is really true."

So on Saturday we joined Kamau and rode our bikes the eight miles to the Mutitu police station. A nice police officer asked what we wanted.

Matt explained and asked if they had brought in any abandoned vehicles. The policeman nodded. "Actually we have quite a few. And we have no time to search for the owners. It's common for thieves to rob a house, drive away in the car, and leave it on some back road." He took us behind the police station. About eight cars sat in the parking area.

"That's the car we're looking for!" Matt pointed to Brad's charcoal gray VW bug in the middle of the line. "KRY 743. That's his license plate."

The policeman smiled. "Tell your friend to bring a copy of his stolen car report from your Rugendo Police Post along with his car's registration logbook, and we'll give him his car."

An off-duty policeman who'd been sleeping in the passenger seat of Brad's car sat up, scratched his head, yawned, and stretched before unfolding himself and clambering out of the car.

I said to the policeman who had helped us, "The car was stolen the same night as the money from a church *harambee* was stolen from Rugendo."

"Yes, we have a report of that," the policeman answered. "Isn't a church elder called Baba Kamau suspected?"

"Yes, he's my father," Kamau said, "but if this car was used as a getaway car to carry that money away from Rugendo, it wasn't my father who stole the money."

The policeman nodded wisely. "You're right. This car was found near Gitonga center. My uncle Hinga lives in Gitonga. He says there are two young men who seem to have gotten a lot of money recently. He has mentioned to me several times that he suspects these young men have done something illegal to get their money."

"Hinga!" I said. "Is that the same Hinga who works as a forest guard near the Thiririka River?"

The policeman nodded. I went on, "He guided our fishing trip last week. And when my dad gave him a magazine, Hinga said he wanted to show two young men a story about a thief who became a Christian in jail."

The policeman smiled. "Hinga told me he'd shown them some magazine story and the two young men became very nervous. Now that you boys have told us that this old Volkswagen came from Rugendo, I think we have enough information to investigate these two young men and find out why they suddenly have so much money to spend. I think with questioning we can prove those young men stole the church *harambee* money from Rugendo and this car as well."

We rode off on our bikes toward Rugendo, stopping at a *chai* house for our favorite snack—*chai* and *mandazi*. As we dunked the greasy square *mandazi* doughnuts in the sweet, milky tea, Matt said, "I can't wait to get back to Rugendo with the news that we found Brad's car. Can you imagine? It was stolen and used as a getaway car."

"I'm glad the real thieves who stole the church *harambee* money will be caught and my dad won't be blamed anymore," Kamau said.

"I think it's time we made you an official member of the Rugendo Rhinos, Kamau," Matt said. "You're our friend. You helped us solve a mystery. You've even visited our tree house. Does everyone agree?"

I reached out to shake Kamau's hand. "Welcome to the Rugendo Rhinos," I said. Dave and Jon congratulated Kamau as well.

We finished drinking our *chai* and rode off to Rugendo to tell everyone what we'd discovered. First we went to Brad and told him where he could find his car. We got my dad and went together to Kamau's house where we told our story. Kamau hugged his dad when they heard the news. Baba Kamau gripped each one of us in a handshake that almost crushed our hands in his massive grip. My dad promised to drive Brad and Baba Kamau to the Mutitu police station with a policeman from Rugendo to clear everything up.

After that we went in search of the Cheetahs. They weren't at

Jill's house, but we found them near the school playground. Matt sauntered up, and we followed. "Guess what we found," Matt taunted.

"We already know you found a group of thieves taking apart stolen cars," Jill answered, "so you don't have to keep on bragging about it. Remember, we Cheetahs helped solve a case as well."

"Yeah, Cheetahs are the best," gloated Freddie from a massive branch in a pepper tree.

Matt smiled. "We found something more. We found Brad's VW bug," he announced.

"Where?" Jill asked. "In pieces in a spare parts garage?"

Matt shook his head. "Nope. Tell 'em, Dean."

So I told them about how we'd followed my hunch and found Brad's VW bug at the Mutitu police station and how it had been used to help the men who'd stolen the *harambee* money to escape. "Those thieves will be caught soon, and Kamau's dad's name will be cleared. And Brad's already gone to collect his bug," I finished.

"I can't believe it," Jill said. "The guys who stole Brad's Volkswagen were really the men who took the *harambee* money?"

Dave stepped forward. "I've made a calculation," he said in his brainy kind of way. "You Cheetahs helped round up a gang of car thieves and international car smugglers. We Rhinos uncovered a gang that stole cars at gunpoint and tore them apart to sell the spare parts. And now we Rhinos discovered how Brad's bug was stolen and used as a getaway vehicle, and we've managed to help Brad recover it. According to my count that means the Rugendo Rhinos solved two car mysteries while the Cheetahs only solved one."

"Good counting, Dave," Matt said. "I guess that shows the

Rugendo Rhinos are the best club at solving mysteries. Good-bye, Cheetahs." Matt turned and we followed him down the path.

Jill and the Cheetahs didn't seem to have an answer, but as we reached the outdoor basketball court Jill shouted out to us, "Just wait until there's another mystery to be solved. We'll beat you then. You'll see."